HANNAH'S HERO

MARGERY SCOTT

CLOVER RIDGE PRESS

HANNAH'S HERO

MAIL-ORDER BRIDES OF SAPPHIRE SPRINGS

Miranda

Audra

Kathryn

Elise

Laura

Cassie

BRIDES OF COLDWATER CREEK

Josie

Sally

Anna

Beth

Willa

OTHER HISTORICAL ROMANCES

Emma's Wish

Wild Wyoming Wind

Rose: Bride of Colorado

MEDICAL ROMANCES

The Surgeon's Homecoming

Stranded with the Surgeon

The Firefighter and the Lady Doc

ROMANTIC SUSPENSE

A Time for Secrets
No One to Tell
The Stranger She Knows
A Question of Guilt

CHAPTER 1

Hannah Blakely tugged her knitted shawl tighter around her shoulders. The mountain air had grown cooler in the past hour or so, but she'd been so engrossed in the sketch of the waterfall that she was working on that she hadn't really noticed until now.

Earlier in the afternoon, she'd filled two buckets with wild raspberries from a patch a mile or so down the trail and hung them from the saddle horn with a strap, making a mental note to ride slowly and carefully so they didn't get too badly bruised before she got home. What her sister didn't need, she'd sell to the mercantile in Rocky Ridge. Mr. Todd was always pleased to have fresh fruit and berries to offer his customers.

Then she'd ridden farther up the trail, and for the rest of the afternoon, she'd been sitting on a rock near the riverbank, her sketch pad on her lap, the sun warm on her face, the scent of pine and cedar filling the air around her. Nearby, a waterfall of ice-cold water crashed down from an outcropping in the rocks a hundred feet up into the rocks at the base, then flowed out into a deep pool where she'd spent many summer afternoons as a young girl.

Late afternoon was her favorite time of the day, when the light and shadows became more dramatic as dusk approached. Now, the sun that had warmed her earlier in the day had disappeared, hidden in the dark clouds scudding across the sky.

Seconds later, the first raindrops fell and a sudden gust of wind whipped up, swirling the dried leaves on the ground around her into a small whirlwind.

Quickly, she closed her sketchbook and bounded to her feet, annoyed with herself that she hadn't paid attention to the weather. Now she'd be cold and very wet before she got back to the small ranch where she lived with her sister, her brother-in-law and their two children.

As she hurried to where Dixie, her mare, was tethered to a tree branch, the rain increased, falling harder and faster. The wind drove the rain sideways, lashing at the skin uncovered by her shawl and dress. By the time she stuffed her sketchbook and pencils into the saddlebag and mounted, it was coming down in sheets.

Thunder rumbled in the distance. She flicked the reins to urge Dixie to move faster, but at the same time she knew she couldn't allow the mare to go faster than a walk without risking injury. Hannah had been in the barn the day Dixie was born, and she'd fallen in love with the foal immediately. She'd been thrilled when Archie, her sister's husband, had given her the foal to raise as her own. She'd never do anything that could hurt the gentle animal.

The trail was treacherous, a river of mud that squelched under Dixie's hooves. Loose gravel and stones slid away with every step. Thunder boomed again, closer now. A streak of lightning split the sky a few seconds later.

For a few moments, she considered stopping and sheltering under a tree until the storm passed. Then she remembered hearing about one of her family's neighbors when she was a girl. Caught in a freak summer storm, the Scotsman had been waiting under a tree for the rain to stop. He'd died when lightning hit the tree he was standing under. She'd never quite understood how lightning hitting a tree could kill someone, and when she'd asked at the time, she'd never gotten a real answer. All she'd been told was never to stand under a tree during a storm.

No, she decided, she'd have to keep going. Getting home as quickly as she could was the only choice she had. It would just take much longer than usual to reach to the warmth and safety of the Circle J ranch house.

Dixie faltered, slipping in the mud, and Hannah's heart leaped into her throat. She noticed her knuckles were white from holding the reins so tightly, so she forced herself to loosen her grip, letting the mare pick her way down the mountain trail at her own pace.

Suddenly, thunder cracked directly overhead. Startled, Dixie let out a snort and a sound Hannah knew meant the horse was terrified. A split second later, she reared up.

Before Hannah had a chance to tighten her grip again on the reins, she felt herself being tossed out of the saddle.

She heard herself scream as she flew through the air. Moments later, twigs and brush clawed at her skin as she hit the ground, landing in a heap on the side of the trail.

Her breath whooshed out of her lungs and pain ricocheted through her. Her vision blurred and faded until the world went black.

Marshal Kirby Matheson swore. The ache in his knee that morning had warned him rain was coming, but he'd ignored it and ridden out, anyway. Abel Cooper's trial in Denver wasn't scheduled for a few days, which would give Kirby a day or two to stop and visit with his brother's family before he continued on. He'd known there'd be rain at some point during the ride, but the way his knee acted up when it was damp didn't tell him when or how much rain there would be. He'd looked at the sky and figured if there was going to be a real storm, he'd at least get as far as Rocky Ridge before it started. He'd been wrong.

He hadn't ridden more than a few miles when the sky had darkened to the color of slate. The breeze had picked up to a raging wind, and torrential rain jabbed at his skin like tiny spears as he rode.

Thunder rumbled nearby and lightning streaked across the sky. He tensed. He'd never liked storms. He'd almost been struck by lightning once when he was a boy. He remembered how terrified he'd been, and his insides still clenched tight whenever he was caught outside during a lightning storm. It had happened a few times over the years and even though he could feel the tension in his body when he had to go outside in a storm, his own feelings had never stopped him from doing his job. Didn't mean he'd ever gotten over it, though, and if he had any choice, he stayed inside until the storm was over.

He'd taken this trail once or twice before, and if his memory was as good as it usually was, he guessed there should be a ranch house just over the ridge ahead.

Anxious to get himself and his horse out of danger, he urged the horse forward. Sure enough, as he crested the ridge, he saw a house in the valley and the faint glow of a lamp in the window.

A few minutes later, he slowed Gypsy, his bay gelding, in front of a log house with a wide porch. He hadn't even really reined the horse to a stop when the door flew open and a woman rushed outside onto the porch.

"Hannah—" She stopped suddenly, her dark blue eyes widening when she saw him. She tucked a few strands of reddish-blonde hair into the knot at the nape of her neck. "You're not Hannah."

Kirby dismounted. "No, ma'am, I'm not. The name's Kirby Matheson. I'm a US marshal from Cedar Valley, on my way to Denver when I got caught in the storm. Mind if I step onto the porch out of the rain?"

"Oh … of course…I apologize for my lack of manners …"

Kirby dismounted and climbed the stairs, then took off his worn brown Stetson. Reaching out into the rain, he shook off the small pool of water that had settled on the brim of his hat before putting it back on his head. Raindrops clung to his hair and dripped down his neck inside his duster.

"Who's Hannah?" he asked, taking note of the tension in the woman's eyes and the fear he'd heard in her voice.

"My baby sister," the woman replied. "I'm so worried. She went out early this afternoon. Her horse came back without her an hour ago."

Kirby scanned the empty pastures around the house. There was no sign of the missing girl. He wasn't surprised the woman was worried. When a horse returned by itself…that usually meant the rider was either hurt or dead.

Tears formed in the woman's eyes, and she wrapped her arms across her chest, her fingers digging into her opposite arms. "I can't leave the children to go and look for her, and Archie … my husband … he went into town this morning to get supplies. I'm not concerned about him. I'm sure he's perfectly safe in town. But Hannah—"

The storm was worsening. Kirby's heart was thumping in his chest, but he tamped down his own fear. The girl was obviously in some kind of trouble, and if somebody didn't go and look for her, she could die out there. If she wasn't dead already, he couldn't help thinking. "Don't worry, ma'am," Kirby said. "I'll go find her."

"But you're already soaked right through—"

"Can't get any wetter," he commented, plastering a smile on his face he didn't feel. "What was she wearing?"

The woman seemed to think for a few moments. "Yellow," she said finally. "Yes, she was wearing a yellow dress."

"Good," he commented. "A bright color will be easier to see in this dim light."

"I—"

"One thing, ma'am," he interrupted. "I'm about half frozen. If you have any hot coffee handy, I'd sure appreciate a cup before I go."

Her face calmed now that she had a mission. "Oh, yes. Come in and I'll get you a cup."

Kirby followed her inside, stopping on the hand-hooked rug by the door and letting the heat from the fire burning in the fireplace wash over him. He was tempted to move closer so he could soak up its warmth, but he'd likely leave puddles all over the woman's floor if he did. He doubted she'd mind under the circumstances, but he stayed where he was, anyway.

A boy he figured was about six or seven years old was sitting in a chair, a book open in his lap. He glanced up when Kirby came inside, but he didn't speak. A girl who looked like a small version of her mother sat beside him. She gave him a tremulous smile, then turned her attention back to the book.

"Here you are," the woman said, crossing back from the kitchen and handing him a pottery mug filled with hot coffee. "I have cream, too, if you prefer."

"Black's fine, ma'am. Thanks." He blew on the coffee before he took a sip. It was strong, just the way he liked it.

He drained the mug as fast as he could without burning his insides, then handed it back to her. "That helped," he said. "Now, I'll be going before it gets dark. Which direction did your sister go?" he asked.

"She said she wanted to draw the waterfall over by Miner's Pass. Do you know where that is?"

He did. "Then she shouldn't be too hard to find since there's a trail that runs up that way."

"I can't thank you enough for braving the storm to go and look for her," the woman said.

"No problem, ma'am," he replied. "All part of the job." He tried to force a smile to his lips, but by the worried frown creasing the woman's forehead, he wasn't sure he succeeded in making her feel any better.

The storm was worsening. Thunder roared overhead. Jagged bursts of lightning streaked across the sky. If Kirby didn't find the missing girl soon, it would be too dark to see anything. And if she was left out there overnight … He refused to let his mind go there.

The waterfall can't be much further, he thought, wiping the rain off his face with his hand, a useless gesture. He still hadn't seen any sign of the girl. Any hoofprints had been washed away by the rain, so there wasn't nothing to track. Had he missed her? Or had she even taken this trail? There was no way to know. He glanced up at the sky. He had maybe another half hour or so before he'd have to give up, but until then, he'd keep going.

Even over the wind bellowing along the trail, he heard the rush of water as it crashed against the rocks at the bottom of Miner's Falls. The trail was nothing but mud now, and several times Gypsy slipped, almost throwing him off as the horse struggled to keep his balance.

Kirby rounded a bend, and a flash of yellow

almost hidden in the brush beside the trail a few yards away caught his eye.

He couldn't tell at that distance if what he was seeing was a piece of fabric, but he hoped he'd gotten lucky and it was the girl he was looking for.

In an instant, he dismounted. He hated to take the extra few seconds to loop Gypsy's reins around a tree branch, but it was necessary. Gypsy had come by his name honestly, and there was no doubt in Kirby's mind that the horse would wander away if he got the chance.

And if that happened, and assuming Kirby had found Hannah, they'd both be in trouble.

He raced toward the sliver of color, stomping through the mud and dead scrub until he reached a mound of yellow fabric half-buried in the brush that could only belong to Hannah.

She was lying on her stomach in the dirt, her head turned to the side. If she'd landed a few inches over, her face would have been submerged in a puddle and she would have drowned.

She could still be dead, though, he reminded himself. She sure didn't look like she had any life left in her.

A strange sensation filled him as he crouched beside her. The woman had called Hannah her "baby sister", and Kirby had assumed she was much younger than the woman lying here in the dirt. Hannah was no girl, and even though she was splattered with mud, she was still a beautiful woman.

Twigs and pine needles were entwined in her wheat-colored hair. Mud splattered her ghostly-white face and a few freckles dotted her small upturned nose.

She was soaked through, and the thin yellow fabric clung to her breasts. Even the petticoats he knew she'd be wearing under the dress were plastered to her, revealing all her curves. No, Hannah was definitely not a girl.

It occurred to him that he didn't know her last name. In fact, he hadn't even gotten her sister's name. It wasn't proper to address a woman by her given name without permission, but under the circumstances, he didn't think she'd mind too much. "Hannah?"

There was no response. He touched his finger to the side of her neck.

Her skin was cold, and as he searched for the pulse point, he braced himself to feel nothing. But then he felt it—a soft pulse beneath her skin. She was alive!

"Hannah! Can you hear me?"

Her eyelids fluttered and finally opened. She gazed up at him with eyes the color of , but there was no sign that she was aware of him. Any woman in her right mind would panic at waking to find a strange man bending over her.

Her eyes closed. He waited, and a few moments later, they opened again. This time, they narrowed and a frown formed between her dark blue eyes.

"Who …?" she asked, her voice trembling. "What happened?"

"You must have fallen off your horse," he told her. "He came back alone."

"She. Dixie's a mare. Is she okay?"

He had to admit it intrigued him that a woman who'd been lying in the rain and mud for what could be hours was more interested in her horse than in her own condition. But right now, he was more interested in her. "Are you okay?"

"I think so," she replied. "But Dixie … she got spooked by the thunder and threw me. That's never happened before."

Well, at least her brains didn't seem to be addled. That pleased him.

Kirby shrugged. "I'm sorry, I don't know anything about it other than your sister said he … she … came home. I'm sure she's fine, and the sooner we get you home, the sooner you can see for yourself."

She nodded.

"Did you hit your head?" he asked. He hadn't seen any blood, but since she'd been out cold when he arrived, it was possible she had a head injury even though there was no bleeding.

She slowly moved her head from side to side, then looked up at him. "It doesn't hurt … I don't think so …"

"Well, that's good," he said. "You probably fainted from pain or shock."

"Or getting the wind knocked out of me," she

added. "I remember hitting the ground. Hard. And I couldn't catch my breath."

"That might do it, too. Can you feel your toes?" He was worried she might have broken her spine in the fall, in which case she'd be paralyzed for the rest of her life.

She frowned. "I'm not sure. I'm so cold they might have frozen and fallen off. You didn't happen to see them anywhere, did you?"

She tried to smile, but it ended up looking more like a grimace. Kirby couldn't help thinking this was a woman who didn't let bad luck get her down. He didn't know many women like that. Hell, he didn't know many men like that either.

Since she seemed to be trying to be light-hearted, he decided to go along with it. "No toes, unless the birds and squirrels took them before I got here."

"Well, as long as they get put to good use …" She let her voice trail off.

"We need to get you home before we both freeze to death," he said, bringing the subject back to the problem at hand, "but I don't want you to move too much until I make sure you won't injure yourself worse."

He wrapped an arm around her shoulder to help her to sit up. Her skin felt like satin beneath his fingers, but so cold. She gritted her teeth with every movement, and he could see she was holding her breath.

For a few seconds, he waited until she was ready to

try to stand. "Ready?" he asked when her breathing returned to normal.

She nodded. He began to help her to her feet, but as soon as she put weight on her leg, she collapsed and let out a moan. Luckily, he had his arm around her waist to support her so she didn't fall. "My ankle …"

Kirby had no way of knowing if it was broken or sprained. "Can I take a look at it?" He knew it was highly improper for a man to see a woman's ankles, but in this case, it could make a difference. If it was obviously broken, he'd have to come up with some kind of splint to keep it steady until they could get her to a doctor.

She didn't answer immediately, but finally she nodded and lifted the hem of her dress a few inches.

Even through her stockings, Kirby could see her ankle was a bit swollen, but he'd seen worse. He carefully examined it, doing his best not to hurt her. Still, he heard her wince a few times. "It doesn't feel as if it's broken," he said when he was finished, "but I'm not a doctor so I can't say for sure. You should get it looked at as soon as you can just in case."

She nodded. "I will."

"Do you have any pain anywhere else?" he asked.

She looked at the scratches and scrapes covering her arms. "These actually hurt worse than my ankle."

He knew from experience that sometimes a surface wound was more painful than a deep one, at least at first. "Let's get you home then so you can get them cleaned out and put some salve on them."

He half-lifted her off the ground until she managed to slip one foot into the stirrup of Kirby's horse and hoist herself into the saddle. Kirby mounted up behind her.

She held herself stiff, staying as far away from him as she could. He understood that. He was a stranger to her, and a woman with any morals at all would be mortified to find herself in a situation like this.

But she was shivering with cold. Opening his duster, he shifted closer to her so he could wrap her in it as well. For a few seconds, she hesitated but then relaxed against him.

Her soft curves fit perfectly against him, and it only served to remind him how long it had been since he'd held a woman.

He swore at himself. The woman was hurt, and even while his mind was on getting her home safely, his natural instincts were sending him other signals. He only hoped she couldn't tell what her closeness was doing to him.

Hannah sat in the saddle, her hands wrapped around the saddle horn. She felt so weak and unsteady she was sure she'd fall off if she didn't hold on tight.

With one swift movement, the man had swung himself into the saddle behind her. She'd felt him move, and a few seconds later, his body had pressed against hers, hard and warm.

She wanted nothing more than to bury herself in that warmth, but instead she jerked away from the contact and held herself as stiff as possible. Heavens, she didn't even know this man.

"Here," she heard him say behind her as he draped his duster around her shoulders, "lean back against me. This duster isn't big enough for both of us."

Propriety warred with her need for warmth. Propriety lost. She relaxed against his solid muscled chest, relishing the heat coming from his body. His scent, a mixture of leather and rain, filled her nose, and his arms came around her to pick up the reins.

She felt her face flush at the realization that she was sitting in a very intimate position with a man who was a complete stranger to her. Luckily, he couldn't see her face, and it would be too painful to turn her head to see his.

She did recall dark hair and dark eyes, and a chin shadowed by a day's growth of hair but that was all. "I don't even know who you are," she said, "but I do want to thank you for coming to my rescue."

"Kirby Matheson, ma'am," he replied. "I know your name is Hannah, but not your last name."

"It's Blakely. I'm Hannah Blakely."

"Well, Miss Blakely, I'm happy to meet you."

She chuckled then, although it sounded more like a wounded animal than a real laugh. "Under the circumstances, I think it would be all right if you call me Hannah."

"If you call me Kirby."

She nodded. An unusual name, she thought. She'd have to remember to ask him about it once she was warm and dry.

Rain pelted her face mercilessly and wind tore at her hair, but she snuggled tighter, nestled in the man's arms.

Every movement of the horse jolted Hannah until she wanted to cry out, but she clamped her lips shut and held onto the saddle horn, thankful to be alive.

Even though it was late spring and the days were pleasantly warm, the temperature still dropped sharply at night. If he hadn't come along, she never would have survived.

Right now, every muscle in her body ached and she was so tired it took every ounce of energy she had to keep herself upright in the saddle. She'd likely feel even worse in the morning, but she had to get to Silver City to finish the painting she'd been commissioned to do. Canceling was not an option.

It seemed to take forever to crest the ridge and see the familiar scene in front of her, but finally, he slowly steered the horse down the hill and across the pasture toward the ranch house.

CHAPTER 2

*N*ight had fallen. With no moon to guide him, it was only because of the lamplight from the windows and the lantern hanging on a hook on the front porch that Kirby could find his way back to the ranch house where Hannah lived.

Mrs. Jarvis was already waiting on the porch by the time he reined Gypsy in at the bottom of the steps.

"Hannah! You're safe," Mrs. Jarvis cried out, hurrying to take Hannah's hand regardless of the rain still teeming down. She gazed up at Kirby, her eyes filled with gratitude. "I don't know how to thank you."

"Glad I could help, ma'am," he replied. Turning to Hannah, he reached up to help her down.

She was light in his arms, and as he lifted her down, he found himself reluctant to release her. "I'll carry you into the house," he said.

"Why? What's wrong—?"

"It's nothing, Florence," Hannah interrupted. "I hurt my ankle a bit and I have a few scratches, that's all."

"Archie's in the barn. I'll send him to fetch the doctor."

"No!" Hannah twisted in Kirby's arms to stop her sister from going after her brother-in-law. "It's not that bad. I'm sure it's just a little sprain."

With Hannah still in his arms, Kirby climbed the porch steps. Mrs. Jarvis hurried ahead to open the door and then stepped aside so he could take her into the house first. Mrs. Jarvis followed and closed the door behind them.

Again, he paused just inside. Rain dripped off his duster onto the rug. "I don't want to put you down, but I'll leave tracks on the floor if I carry you any further."

Mrs. Jarvis waved away Kirby's concern. "Oh, don't worry about that. Hannah's room is upstairs, if it's not too much trouble to carry her up."

"No problem at all," he replied. If truth be told, he'd be fine with carrying her for miles if it meant he could keep her in his arms a while longer.

"Really, Kirby, I can walk—"

Before she had a chance to protest further, Kirby crossed the parlor to the stairs leading to the second floor of the house.

A small voice piped up from the top of the stairs. "What did you do, Auntie Hannah? What's the man carrying you for?"

"Scoot out of the way, Tommy," Mrs. Jarvis ordered. "Let the marshal take your aunt to her room."

The little boy eyed him warily, but stepped away from the stairs to let Kirby pass. When he reached the top, he gave Hannah a questioning glance. "Which one is yours?"

Hannah pointed to a closed door at the end of a hallway with three other doors leading off it. Mrs. Jarvis followed them, standing back while Kirby carried Hannah down the hall and into the room.

A large four-poster bed covered in a brightly colored patchwork quilt took up most of the room. A dresser with a jug and basin on top sat against one wall and a wardrobe stood against the other.

He was about to set her on the bed when she stopped him. "I'm wet," Hannah said. "Put me down there." She pointed to a rocking chair in one corner.

Kirby gently deposited her in the chair and straightened. He missed having her in his arms, missed breathing in her lavender scent and feeling her breath against his cheek.

Hannah's sister bustled around the room, opening and closing dresser drawers and riffling through the wardrobe while she dug out dry clothes for Hannah.

The boy hovered just outside the door. Florence turned to him. "Billy," she said, "ask your papa to take care of the marshal's horse." She turned back to Hannah.

"That's not necessary, Mrs. Jarvis—" Kirby put in.

"Nonsense," she replied, waving away his objection. "And you should call me Florence. Everyone does. It's too dark to travel now and the storm isn't letting up. You can wait it out right here. I fed the children and Libbie is already asleep. Tommy can sleep in the spare bed in her room and you can take his."

"I don't want to intrude--"

"Don't be silly," she interrupted again. "It's nice to have some company. If you wouldn't mind staying with Hannah in case she needs something while I get some water—"

"Not at all." He was happy to spend as much time with this woman as possible. Something about her appealed to him, something he hadn't felt in a long time.

"I'm fine, Florence. There's no need to fuss," Hannah put in.

Florence gave Kirby a resigned smile. "Too independent for her own good," she muttered. "It'll take too long to heat enough water for a bath, but I do have some water heating on the stove that will take care of most of the mud." Florence hurried out of the room.

Kirby smiled and reached out to pick a dried leaf out of Hannah's hair. She gazed up at him, her dark blue eyes both curious and suspicious at the same time until he showed her the leaf. Then she gave him a smile that put a sparkle in her eyes and showed a tiny dimple at the corner of her mouth.

A sudden urge to taste that dimple—and the rest of her mouth—surged over him. The emotion was so strong he took a step back in case his willpower wasn't strong enough to resist.

Kirby realized how uncomfortable Hannah must be having a man—a stranger—in her private sleeping quarters. "Nice room," he said, his voice sounding loud in the silence. "Did you make the quilt?"

She nodded. "It's made from scraps of clothes I outgrew," she commented. "The pink with the flowers on it was my favorite dress."

"Nice." He couldn't think of anything else to say. Luckily, Florence saved him from having to think of something.

She scurried back into the room with a bowl of hot water, a clean cloth draped over her arm, and a small jar of what he assumed was some kind of salve for Hannah's wounds. "If you don't mind waiting downstairs," she said to Kirby, "I'll help Hannah clean up and change her clothes and then we'll have supper. I have a huge pot of stew on the stove and some fresh-baked biscuits."

Hannah gripped the arms of the rocking chair and tried to stand. "I need to go check on Dixie. She was so terrified when she ran off she might have hurt herself."

Kirby placed a restraining hand on her shoulder. "You need to rest that ankle."

"Dixie's fine," Florence assured her. "Archie took care of her."

"You're sure she's not hurt?"

Florence nodded. "She's fine."

Hannah lowered herself back into the chair. "I can clean up myself if you'll get me some dry clothes out of the wardrobe," she said to Florence. Then she turned her attention to Kirby and grinned. "I promise I won't be long," she said. "You're probably hungry. I know I'm starving."

Hannah waited until the bedroom door closed behind Kirby to get up. Her ankle throbbed, but she managed to undo the tiny pearl buttons on her dress and let it drop in a puddle on the floor.

"He's really very handsome, isn't he?" Florence commented as she crossed to the wardrobe in the corner of the room and took out a lilac dress with white lace trim. She spread it out on the bed.

"I hadn't noticed," Hannah replied. That was a bald-faced lie, and both Hannah and Florence knew it. Unfortunately, her sister knew her too well.

The man was *too* handsome, she thought, from his chestnut hair to the golden flecks in his dark brown eyes to his strong square jaw. But it was more than a handsome face that had affected her. Something about him that she couldn't define attracted her.

Hannah turned away from Florence's disbelieving glance and lifted the washcloth out of the bowl. She wrung it out and carefully began to wipe the dirt and gravel out of the scrapes on her arms.

"Of course you did," Florence contradicted with a smile. "You'd have to be blind not to notice. He's very nice, too," she added. "He didn't have to go back out into the storm to search for you."

"I know that," Hannah muttered.

Florence pulled clean undergarments out of a drawer, then returned to the wardrobe for clean petticoats. "I wonder if he's married."

"I'm sure he probably has a wife and six children waiting for him in Cedar Valley. It doesn't matter, anyway."

"You're not getting any younger—"

Florence's tone was kind, but the truth of the matter was that Hannah wasn't getting any younger. She was twenty-two, past prime marrying age, and with no prospects in sight.

"If he's not married—"

"It doesn't matter." Hannah looked up from patting her arm dry. "You know I would never get involved with a lawman."

"They're not all like—"

"Stop! Please stop!"

"I'm sorry," Florence said, wrapping an arm around Hannah's shoulder and giving her a gentle squeeze. "You know I only want you to be happy."

Hannah did know. She'd moved to the ranch to live with Florence and Archie six years before when her mother had died from the fever that swept the town. Since then, she'd helped around the house and even taken on some of the outside chores to help to repay their generosity. She was happy with her life, but her sister was right. It was past time she was married and had a family of her own.

But even if he was single, the one man she definitely wouldn't consider was the marshal waiting for her downstairs.

Kirby looked up and saw Hannah at the top of the stairs almost an hour later. He'd thought she was beautiful before. Now she was stunning.

She still had scratches and welts on her arms, but she was clean now. Her hair was still damp and was piled on her head, a few loose tendrils framing her pale cheeks.

An image floated into his mind—Hannah, her hair unpinned and her curls tumbling down across her shoulders and down her back. The thought was so strong it made his breath catch in his throat.

She'd changed into a lilac dress with white lace trim that hugged her curves and emphasized her bare neck.

A neck he'd love to feel against his lips. "You look much better," he commented.

"As you do," she replied. "You changed your clothes."

He nodded. While she was upstairs, he'd gone out to the barn, introduced himself to Archie, and changed into dry pants and a shirt he'd pulled out of his saddlebags.

Kirby was afraid she was going to fall if she tried to get down the stairs by herself, so he hurried up to where she was standing.

She had one hand wrapped around the newel post, the other around a cane she'd somehow come up with.

"I'll carry you down," he said. He didn't add that he'd be happy to have her back in his arms for another minute or so.

"I can manage," she announced.

"It's no trouble—"

"No." She gazed at him, determination in her eyes. "I'll do it myself."

His insides clenched. If she fell … "Suit yourself, but if it's all the same to you, I'll stand in front of you just in case."

For a few beats, their gazes met, and he wondered if she'd refuse even that. Finally, she shrugged. "Suit yourself," she said shortly, but Kirby had the feeling she was glad he was there as a buffer.

Slowly, carefully, Hannah hobbled down the stairs until she reached the bottom. Her eyes lit up and a smile of triumph crossed her face. Her breathing was heavy as if she'd run a race, but Kirby thought better of mentioning it.

"Come and eat before it gets cold." Florence's voice came from the dining room where she was dishing out bowls of stew. A plate of biscuits sat in the middle of the table.

Hannah limped toward the table and tried to pull her chair out with one hand while she held the cane with the other. The chair was so heavy it barely budged.

Kirby hurried to help her and took the cane from her once she was sitting down.

Florence pointed to the chair directly opposite Hannah. "Kirby, you sit there."

Kirby didn't complain. He liked looking at Hannah, at her wide eyes that sparkled in the lamplight. He hated to see the scratches marring her creamy skin, but they were minor and would go away soon.

"Are you feeling better now?" he asked Hannah after Archie said the blessing.

She nodded. "Much, thanks. My ankle still hurts but I can wiggle my toes and it holds my weight even if it does hurt like blazes, so I'm pretty sure it's not broken. I'm sure it'll be fine in a day or two."

Kirby wasn't so sure she wasn't oversimplifying her injury, but she seemed like the kind of woman who wouldn't take kindly to his opinion. So he kept quiet.

"What happened to the berries?" Hannah asked Florence between bites of her stew. "I picked two buckets of wild raspberries."

Florence shook her head. "I'm sorry. They were mostly juice by the time Dixie got back here."

Disappointment clouded Hannah's eyes. "I was hoping to sell some of them to Mr. Todd."

"There will be more berries to pick once the weather clears."

"That's true. I just hope I'll have time to order the artists' kit I want from the catalog and get it before fall."

Kirby was intrigued. "You're an artist?"

She nodded, and before she had a chance to answer, Florence spoke up. "Hannah got all the artistic talent in the family. Her paintings are wonderful, and they even did a story about her in *The Rocky Mountain News.*"

Kirby was impressed. It was unusual for a newspaper to feature a woman in an article. "I'd like to see some of your work."

Hannah's face flushed with color, as if she was embarrassed. She lowered her head and took a sip from the water glass in front of her. "It's not that good."

"Nonsense. You're far too modest," Archie contradicted, pointing to two paintings on the wall near the fireplace. "Hannah painted those."

"Do you mind?" Kirby asked, making a move to rise from the table to take a closer look at the two portraits.

Hannah shrugged, but it was enough for him. He quickly got up and crossed to take a closer look at the portrait of Tommy and another child with the same reddish-blonde hair as Florence. "They're beautiful," he commented. "I assume this is Tommy's sister," he added, pointing to the toddler in the painting.

Florence chuckled. "Yes, that's Libbie. She's asleep now. You'll meet her in the morning and I guarantee you'll be exhausted within an hour."

Kirby laughed, then rejoined them at the table. "You aren't the law in Rocky Ridge, Marshal," Archie said when he'd settled back in his chair and was finishing his meal "What brings you out this way?"

"That's right." Kirby mopped up the last of the gravy with a biscuit and popped it into his mouth. After he swallowed, he continued. "I'm a US marshal in Cedar Valley. I'm on my way to Denver to testify at a trial."

Archie's brows lifted, but that wasn't what caught Kirby's attention. The half-smile on Hannah's face disappeared.

"Then you'll return to Cedar Valley?" Florence asked.

Kirby shook his head. "Not right away. The accused man, Abel Cooper, is one of a gang of outlaws who've been robbing banks, mostly in Kansas and Wyoming Territory. A few weeks ago, they robbed the bank in Cedar Valley. Abel's brother, Jubel, got killed during the robbery, but not before he killed two women who happened to be in the bank at the time. His other brother, Owen, escaped as well as two other members of the gang."

"I heard about that," Archie said.

"Abel got caught near Denver when a bank teller who'd worked in a bank in Kansas happened to see him in a shop in Denver. Two are dead, but Owen is still out there. Once the trial is over, I'm going after him and taking him in."

Kirby noticed that Hannah's bright eyes narrowed slightly and she seemed to stiffen as he was talking. She was obviously upset.

"Your family doesn't mind you being gone so much?" Florence asked.

Kirby's chest clenched as it always did when he thought about his family. "Don't have much family left, ma'am," he replied. "Just my brother and his wife and daughters. The rest of my family is gone now."

"I'm sorry."

"I've been on my own for a long time," he commented. "But it's me who should be apologizing. I shouldn't be talking about outlaws and robbing and killing at the supper table with ladies present."

Florence got up and began to clear the plates. "Oh, please don't apologize, Marshal. It's good to have company and hear about what's going on in the rest of the world. Now, who would like a piece of pie?"

Hannah rose and gripped the cane that had been resting against the table. "No, thanks. I'm going upstairs. Goodnight, everyone."

Kirby watched her walk away, her lips pressed tightly together, the determination in her eyes. She was limping badly, but he let her go. He'd obviously said or did something that had upset her. He only wished he knew what it was.

CHAPTER 3

Dawn barely lit Hannah's bedroom when she woke the next morning, but at least the rain pounding on the roof had stopped at some point during the night. At times, it had sounded as if the roof was about to cave in on top of her.

She lifted her arms out from beneath the patchwork quilt on her bed and examined her arms. The scratches and scrapes were still red and sore, but the smaller ones already seemed to be healing. Of course, it was early yet, she told herself. It was still possible that infection could set in.

Tucking them back under the quilt, she tugged the quilt around her neck and snuggled lower until she warmed up. She'd like to stay here all day, she thought, but she couldn't. She had responsibilities, and one thing Hannah prided herself on was that she never shirked her responsibilities.

She had to get to Silver City to finish the painting

she'd been commissioned to do. She estimated it would only take two or three more days to put the finishing touches to it and she was running out of time. Her client, Millicent Grover, was paying her well to recreate her mother's childhood home. The painting was a birthday gift for Mrs. Grover's mother and had to be finished before the party Mrs. Grover was hosting the next weekend. If she didn't finish the painting this week, there wouldn't be time to have it framed and wrapped before the party.

Every muscle in Hannah's body protested when she tried to climb out of bed. How was it possible to feel even worse today than she had the evening before?

She shivered as she hobbled to the window. Pulling back the curtain, she looked outside. There wasn't even a sliver of sunshine in the clouds anywhere, and the yard was a sea of mud and puddles. Riding to Silver City would be unpleasantly cold and damp, and by the look of the sky, there was no guarantee she wouldn't get caught in another storm.

But at least it wasn't raining right now, she thought as she washed herself and put on a blue cotton shirtwaist. She wrapped a matching shawl around her shoulders and picked up the carpetbag she'd packed the night before.

The aroma of frying bacon reached her nose when she opened her bedroom door. Her stomach rumbled and she realized she was hungry. Even though she'd eaten supper the evening before, having Kirby Matheson sitting right across from her had done something to her insides. For some reason she couldn't explain, his presence had affected her to the point she'd lost her appetite.

Laughter coming from behind a closed door caught Hannah's attention. Tommy and Libbie were playing inside their bedroom. For a moment, she was tempted to open the door, but decided against it. Better to leave well enough alone, she thought, a smile creeping across her lips.

She hobbled down the stairs, her ankle throbbing with each step. Still, it wasn't quite as painful as the day before, so she was thankful for that. She paused for a moment in front of the fireplace in the main room to warm up before heading into the kitchen.

Florence was alone, and Hannah couldn't help wondering if the marshal had already left. She wouldn't ask, though. Florence would think she was interested in the man. Which she wasn't, she told herself. "I'll do the eggs," she offered, taking a bowl off a shelf near the stove.

"Better make extra," Florence said as Hannah cracked eggs into a bowl. "The marshal is out helping Archie with chores."

Well, Hannah thought, that answered the question she'd been pondering. He was still there, still so handsome, and likely still affecting her more than she liked to admit. And he obviously wasn't the type of man who'd sit and let others wait on him. Another point in his favor, she supposed. If she cared, which she didn't.

She'd seriously considered waiting another day before riding to Silver City, but the sooner she got away from Kirby, the better. "I'll be leaving for Silver City right after breakfast," she said.

Florence looked up from keeping an eye on the bacon in the skillet. "Are you sure that's wise? You're hurt, and the weather—"

"I don't need my ankle to paint," Hannah replied with a smile. "And the weather might not clear for days. I made a commitment to Mrs. Grover. I don't want to let her down."

"I understand that, but—"

Hannah crossed to the stove and wrapped an arm around Florence's shoulders. "I know you worry, but honestly, I'm fine, Florence. Really. I am."

Florence gave her a faint smile and nodded. Hannah returned to the worktable and picked up a fork, whisking the eggs until they were light and frothy.

Just then, the door opened and Archie walked in, a load of firewood cradled in his arms. Kirby followed, carrying two buckets of water. While Archie took the firewood and stacked it in the hod beside the fireplace, Kirby brought the water buckets into the kitchen.

"Good morning, Hannah," he said, giving her a smile that made her nerve endings tingle. "How's the ankle this morning?"

Hannah tamped down the urge to return his smile. "It's fine," she replied shortly, not happy with how his presence affected her. Then, remembering her manners, muttered, "Thank you for asking."

"That's good to hear." Turning to Florence, he said, "I'm happy to pour this into a pot for you. It's heavy."

Florence beamed. "Why, thank you, Marshal. The pot's right over there."

Hannah couldn't help watching him as he crossed the kitchen, her gaze sliding to his corded forearms lifting the buckets of water with seemingly no effort at all. His dark hair curled against the collar of his shirt. The thought that she'd love to see what it felt like to run her fingers through that hair popped into her mind.

Furious with herself, she beat the eggs even harder.

"Breakfast will be ready in a few minutes," Florence told him. "That is, if Hannah ever stops whipping the eggs and cooks them," she added with a chuckle.

Hannah gave her sister a murderous look, but crossed to the stove and poured the eggs into another skillet.

Yes, Hannah thought, all she had to do was suffer through breakfast and then she'd be rid of the marshal forever.

~

Prickly female, Kirby thought a few minutes later when they were all seated at the table. He'd first noticed it when he'd asked about her ankle. People were often a bit short-tempered when they were hurt. Kirby knew that. Still, he sensed it was more than just discomfort from her injuries. What annoyed him more was that he cared why she was suddenly being so unfriendly.

"I should be back by Tuesday at the latest," he heard Hannah say. "It should only take a few days to finish up."

"I still think you should wait," Florence put in, "especially right now. You've been hurt and you shouldn't be going off by yourself."

Hannah shook her head. "I'll be fine. I don't want to wait and then have to rush to finish and not do the best job I possibly can. Besides, I've ridden to Silver City a hundred times by myself."

Kirby was pretty sure that was an exaggeration and she was only trying to make her point.

"Wait a minute." Florence's eyes brightened. "The marshal—".

"Leave her be, Florence," Archie admonished. "She's a grown woman. She knows how you feel about her going all that way alone but it's her decision."

Florence sighed, then reached over and squeezed Hannah's hand. "I'll miss you, but knowing I probably wouldn't be able to change your mind, I packed you some lunch."

"Where you goin', Auntie Hannah?" Tommy looked up at Hannah. A milk mustache covered his upper lip.

Kirby had been wondering that himself.

"Silver City," Hannah replied. "But I'll be back soon, and then we'll finish that book we started reading the other night."

Tommy jerked his head in Kirby's direction. "You going with him?"

"No. I'm going alone." She drained her coffee and stood up. "And I'd better get started so I get there before dark."

Kirby couldn't stop himself. "I'd be happy to go with you, in case you run into any trouble," he heard himself say. "I'm heading to Denver, anyway. I have to go right past Silver City on the way."

She turned to face him. "I prefer to travel alone."

"Your ankle—"

"Will be fine," she insisted. "I don't need anyone to look after me."

Florence got up and crossed to the counter that ran the length of the kitchen. "If the marshal is going in the same direction, wouldn't it be nice to have a little company?"

"No. It wouldn't." She stared at Kirby, her dark blue eyes daring him to protest.

It seemed Hannah Blakely was a fiercely independent woman, Kirby thought as she gave him a curt farewell nod and picked up the sack of food her sister had prepared for her. Then she said goodbye to her family and hurried out.

By early afternoon, Hannah was sorry she hadn't waited an extra day. Her body ached, and she realized it was going to take longer to reach Silver City than it usually did.

Although it wasn't raining and a watery sun was doing its best to shine through the clouds, the air was damp, seeping through her clothes to thoroughly chill her. Parts of the trail had dried, leaving ruts where riders and wagons had gone before.

Hannah was afraid to let Dixie move at more than a walk because of the uneven ground, and she estimated it would be dark by the time she reached the outskirts of Silver City at the rate she was going.

She'd stopped in a clearing off the trail where the river was shallow to eat lunch and let Dixie rest and get her fill of water. As she was packing her saddlebags, she heard what sounded like hoofbeats.

Her heart skittered behind her ribs. She wasn't afraid, well, not really. Still, she was well aware she was a woman alone in the wilderness. She wasn't sure the unseen rider was heading toward her, but just in case, she picked up the rifle she'd leaned against a tree when she'd dismounted.

She aimed the rifle toward the sound. Her body grew tense. Her breaths shortened. The hoofbeats grew louder. The leaves on the trees rustled and moments later, the horse and rider came into view.

Kirby Matheson!

"What are you doing here?" she asked, unable to keep the anger out of her voice. "Do you realize I could have blown your head off?"

He had the audacity to smile. "I gave you credit for at least waiting to see who it was before you pulled the trigger."

"I still could," she pointed out, but lowered the rifle to her side.

"I suppose that's true."

"You haven't answered my question," she said. "Why are you here? Are you following me?"

He shook his head. "I told you I was headed to Denver, but I'm stopping to visit my brother and his family on the way. This is a good spot for a rest. Did you think you were the only one who knew about this place?"

Of course he'd be taking the same trail, Hannah thought. He'd mentioned that at breakfast, and it was the most direct route between the Circle J and Denver. "Well … no. I just didn't expect to see you again, that's all."

He dismounted and took his horse's reins, guiding him down to the riverbank. "That's why I offered to go with you," he said. "How are you holding up?"

Right now, she wanted nothing more than to crawl into bed and sleep for hours. "Fine. Why wouldn't I be?"

He gave her a look that told her he didn't believe her, but he had the good sense not to comment. "No reason. Just thought after your tumble yesterday you might have some aches and pains."

She turned away and continued to pack the saddlebags with the wrappings from her lunch. When she was finished, she put her good foot in the stirrup. The thought of another few hours of riding made her feel like crying, but she had no choice at this point. "I'd better be moving along, otherwise I won't get to Silver City today."

"Wait a minute," Kirby called out from behind her.

She turned to see him coming toward her. He stopped a few feet away. "Look, I don't know what I did to upset you so much, but whatever it was, I'm sorry."

"You didn't do anything—" she began.

"Then why are you so hellbent on traveling by yourself?" he asked. "Surely you know that it's safer— and the time passes a lot quicker—with company. I'd like to get to know you better."

She couldn't tell him she didn't want to travel with him because she was finding him far too handsome, too kind, too … everything. She couldn't tell him she'd like to get to know him better, too, if only he wasn't a lawman.

She knew what caring about a lawman could do to a person.

"Let's ride together," he said. The tone of his

voice sent a ripple of awareness through her. She couldn't say no.

"Well … all right," she agreed. "I suppose it couldn't hurt."

Physically, it couldn't hurt. Emotionally … well, that remained to be seen, but as long as she didn't let herself like him too much, she'd be fine.

They rode in silence for a while, but as the afternoon wore on, Kirby started asking her about her art, figuring she'd be more likely to talk about that than anything really personal. "When did you realize you could draw?" he asked.

She looked over at him and shrugged. "I don't know. I don't remember a time when I didn't draw. Whether it was good or not, I can't say."

Silence threatened again, but Kirby wasn't going to allow the conversation to die. It was one of the few times she'd answered him with more than a one or two-word reply. "I'm sure it was good. Did you study or did it come naturally?"

For a moment, he didn't think she was going to answer, but finally, she spoke. "Archie's family comes from Philadelphia. A few months after Florence and him got married, Archie decided they should take a trip back east so his family could meet her. Archie thought she might be worried, being alone without anybody she knew, so he asked if I'd like to go, too."

He sensed she wasn't finished answering, so he waited patiently until she was ready to go on.

"It was wonderful," she said. Her voice took on a dreamlike quality that warmed him. "They took me to an exhibition at the Pennsylvania Academy of the Fine Arts. I'd never seen paintings by real artists before. At the time, I would have loved to stay—they allowed women to study there - but that was impossible."

"Maybe one day you can go back."

She looked over at him then. "Maybe, but I'm happy with my life the way it is."

That surprised him. Most young women he'd ever known couldn't wait to marry and have a family. "You don't want a husband and children?"

She shrugged. "I suppose so, but it becomes more and more unlikely with every passing day."

"Hannah, this might be too forward of me to say, but you're a beautiful woman. I'm sure you could have your pick of any single man in Rocky Ridge if you wanted one."

She blushed again and looked away.

Silence fell around them. The sun had broken through a short time before, but daylight was already starting to fade. They were still a few miles away from Silver City.

"I don't think we're going to reach Silver City before dark," he said.

She didn't speak for quite some time, her gaze

straight ahead to Miner's Pass. Then she looked up at the sky. "It's not that far."

At breakfast that morning, she'd said she'd made the trip between Rocky Ridge and Silver City many times, so surely she knew they wouldn't get there before night fell. He suspected she just didn't want to admit it. "It's too far to get there before dark, and I don't think we should risk getting caught in Miner's Pass at night."

"Why not?"

"There's no shelter in the pass if there's another storm. And then there are the bears, and the coyotes, and the mountain lions—"

"Then what do you suggest we do?"

"We can make camp in one of the caves near here and start out at sunrise."

Her eyes widened. "Camp here? Both of us? Together? In a cave?"

"Got a better idea?"

"Well … no … but … a cave? How do you know where the caves are?"

"I grew up near here," he told her. "I roamed these woods and trails every day when I was a boy."

"But … what about the animals?"

"I'll build us a fire at the entrance. That should keep any intruders out."

Hannah's teeth worried her lower lip. He couldn't help staring, his mind wandering to the thought of tasting those lips.

She fascinated him. Beautiful, talented, and with a

mind of her own. A woman who refused to be depen-dent on a man. He'd never met a woman like her before, and he was intrigued by her. He'd admit to himself that he wanted her, wanted to kiss her, touch her, and so much more. But what bothered him to admit to himself was that he was starting to like her more than any other woman he'd ever known.

CHAPTER 4

annah couldn't believe she was actually agreeing to spend the night in a cave with Kirby Matheson. What was she thinking?

But what else could she do? She could go on alone, just like she'd done every other time she'd made the trip between the Circle J Ranch and Silver City.

She hated to admit that Kirby was right. She wouldn't make it out of the pass before night fell, and the thought of spending the night outside by herself sent a sliver of fear scurrying up her spine.

No, she realized, she needed him. She sucked in a calming breath and nodded. "Will we be warm enough?" she asked. She still hadn't forgotten how cold she'd been the day before and she had no wish to ever experience that again.

"We'll be sheltered from wind, and some of the heat from the fire should warm the inside of the cave enough that we won't freeze." He glanced up at the gathering dusk. "If we don't ride a little faster, though, we won't get there before dark, and then I won't be able to see to gather enough wood to build us a fire."

She nodded, then urged Dixie into a trot, following Kirby down the trail for a few minutes before he veered off into a stand of trees. A damp musty smell mixed with cedar and pine reached her nose, and the only sounds she heard were those of twigs snapping beneath their horses' hooves.

It didn't take long before he reined in his horse near an opening at the base of the mountain and dismounted.

He looped his horse's reins around a branch. "Wait here while I make sure it's safe," he said, his voice taking on a tone that brooked no argument.

Hannah wasn't about to protest, anyway. She had no desire to go exploring where wild animals could be lurking. At the very least, she assumed any cave would be home for rodents and insects, and maybe even a rattlesnake or two.

Still, she couldn't help feeling a little worried about being left alone. "Where are you going?"

"The cave's right through here," he said, turning away and tearing at the brush until he disappeared from view.

Hannah's chest tightened. If he got hurt … She tried to reason with herself that she was concerned about his safety only because she'd be left alone, but even as she tried to convince herself, she knew that wasn't the whole truth.

She hated to admit it, but she liked him. Yes, he was handsome. He was obviously brave, too, to be a lawman. He believed in justice, and was willing to risk his life for his beliefs. And he was kind. He'd proven that the day before, and now he was going out of his way to make sure she was safe for the night.

But she couldn't let herself like him, she reminded herself. He was a lawman. She'd seen what loving a lawman had done to her mother, and the day her father died, she'd made a vow to herself never to love a man who earned his living with a gun.

A rustling in the brush startled Hannah. She gripped the rifle and pointed it, her finger trembling on the trigger. A moment later, Kirby came into view.

"You might want to wait until tomorrow to shoot me," he said, unlooping his horse's reins. His voice was gruff, but he had a smile on his face and laughter shone out of his eyes.

His light-hearted tone relaxed Hannah. "But if I shoot you now, the bears and coyotes won't bother me. They'll have you for dinner instead."

He nodded. "You'd be much more appetizing, I'm sure."

Their gazes meshed, and a slow warmth seeped through Hannah's limbs. The way he was looking at her … she'd never experienced such a thing before. Why, he was gazing at her as if he'd like to make a meal out of her himself.

Suddenly, he turned away. "Follow me."

Hannah dismounted, stifling a moan when her ankle twisted on a piece of uneven ground.

She hadn't been quiet enough.

Without a word, Kirby spun around and closed the gap between them. "I'm sorry," he said. "I should have realized it would be hard for you to get to the cave."

Looping Dixie's reins around his forearm, he reached around her and in one smooth motion, whisked her off her feet and into his arms.

She couldn't contain the tiny cry of surprise, but soon found her own arms circling his neck. She couldn't resist threading her fingers through his soft chestnut hair at the nape of his neck. Embarrassed that she'd allowed herself to take such a liberty, she burrowed her face into his neck. His scent, so uniquely his, filled her. His heartbeat sounded against her ear.

She hated that she liked the feel of his arms around her. She hated that she liked feeling protected and cared for. She hated that his solid chest against her softness made her feel strangely warm and languid.

And she hated most that this man—this *lawman*—was the man who made her feel these things.

Kirby swore to himself as he carried Hannah into the cave and set her gently down on a stone near the back. What was he doing? He needed to stay away from her, away from her sweet lavender scent, away from the feel of her soft skin, away from the rare smile that turned his insides upside down.

The air was musty and damp, and he saw Hannah's pert nose scrunch up at the smell. She shivered and wrapped her arms around herself against the chill, but she didn't complain.

"I'm going to take care of the horses and gather some wood to build a fire," he said. He didn't like to leave her alone, but he wouldn't be far away. "Do you need anything before I go?"

She grinned. "My rifle," she replied. "I promise I won't shoot you, as long as you don't come back looking like a bear."

"Well, since you promise …" He returned her smile, taking note that she looked exhausted and she was likely in pain but still held her light attitude. His admiration for her grew. "I'll be back as quick as I can, and if you do run into any trouble, I'll be close by."

He left Hannah in the cave and went outside. A cool wind whistled through the trees, and he noticed dusk was quickly falling. If he didn't hurry, it would be too dark to see anything. Quickly, he unsaddled the horses and tied them securely to a tree branch before he took the saddles into the cave before he went in search of kindling and firewood.

Because of the storm the day before, he had no trouble finding enough wood to keep a fire lit the whole night. He was worried that the wood might be too wet to burn so he took an extra few minutes to search out spots where he hoped the air had dried it enough.

With the fire built near the entrance to the cave, he struck a match against the sole of his boot and held it against a small piece of kindling. For a few seconds, he thought he'd failed, but then a tiny flame flickered, and within seconds, the fire grew, sending heat into the cave and sparks into the night sky.

The fire gave some light to the interior of the cave, casting a golden glow on Hannah's face. The sight made his breath catch in his throat, and for a few seconds, he could do nothing but stare.

Her pale hair glimmered and her eyes sparkled. There was no doubt she was even more beautiful in the glow of the firelight, but it was more than just beauty that drew him to her. There was something about her he couldn't name, an undefinable force he couldn't resist.

Desire surged through him, and heat that had nothing to do with the fire outside filled his veins. He wanted her. But as much—or even more—than his physical desire, he wanted to know everything about her, to protect her. To just be with her. Always.

"Come and sit down." Her soft voice pierced his wayward thoughts. It was only then he noticed she'd been busy while he was gone.

She was sitting on one of the saddle blankets she'd spread out on the floor of the cave. Paper-wrapped sandwiches, cheese and cookies were laid out, as if she was hosting a picnic. Water canteens sat at the edge of the blanket.

"I hope you don't mind," she said. "I got these out of your saddlebags. I only had a few cookies left."

He crossed the cave and sat down beside her. "I don't mind. I'm hungry. I haven't eaten anything since I left your sister's ranch."

"Oh …" A slow flush came over her face. "I'm so sorry. I wasn't thinking … I'd already eaten most of what she packed for me and I was about to leave when you arrived … It didn't occur to me that you hadn't. Why didn't you say something?"

At the time, he hadn't realized they wouldn't reach Silver City before nightfall. "If I'd taken the time to eat, we wouldn't have gotten this far," he replied.

He was glad they'd had to stop, though. He couldn't deny it. He wanted the extra time to spend with Hannah, to get to know the woman who was making him think about home, and family, and settling down, instead of spending most of his nights alone on the trail of one outlaw or another.

He'd only known her for one day, so how was it possible he felt this way?

While Kirby ate, Hannah only nibbled on a piece of cheese.

"There's plenty of food," he pointed out. "You must be hungry, too."

Hannah shook her head. "This is fine. I would love a cup of coffee, though," she added with a smile.

Kirby grinned. "Next time we go on a trip, I'll be sure to bring a coffeepot."

She blushed as her gaze met Kirby's for a moment before she looked away. "When is the trial?"

"Day after tomorrow," he responded.

"If my accident hadn't prevented you from going on, you would already be in Denver. Did you have other plans for your time there?"

"I'd planned to stop and see my brother and his family on the way."

"Oh, that's right … You said he has a ranch not far from here. You won't have time now," she said, getting up and starting to clear away the remnants of their meal. "I'm sorry—"

"It's not your fault, and I'm glad I had company. It gets lonely out on the trail sometimes."

"I'm sure it does." She stuffed the empty wrappings into her saddlebag and limped closer to the entrance of the cave. Rubbing her hands together, she held her palms out to the fire. Then she turned to face him. "Why do you do it?"

"It's my job."

"Did you always want to be a lawman?"

"No." He couldn't really explain why he'd taken the job. He'd been without a purpose, wandering from town to town, taking odd jobs wherever he found them. He didn't really know why he hadn't settled down on the piece of land his father had left him the way his brother had on his. The parcels were good grazing land that butted against each other, a river running through them to make sure they'd always have enough water for a herd.

"I was passing through Cedar Valley. I was in the saloon one night, playing poker with a few hands who'd come into town. Someone ran in and said the marshal had died."

"What happened to him? Did someone kill him?"

Kirby shook his head. "No. He just died."

"And?"

"The next day, I was in the mercantile. The mayor happened by, was talking to the owner. They offered me the job. I didn't have a good reason to turn it down. It paid better and it was easier work. Been doing it ever since."

"Why do you do it? Why do you want to live your life knowing at any moment you might be killed?"

"I don't think about that. I'm trying to make my town a safe place so people can raise their families without fear."

"What about your own family's fear? Don't you think your brother worries about you when you're off chasing outlaws?"

"I suppose he might. Somebody's got to do it or outlaws would rule the world. Where there's nobody to uphold the law, there'd be more bloodshed and nobody would be safe, not even your own family."

"Why you?"

"Why not me?"

Because you're tired of spending your nights sleeping on the cold ground when you're tracking outlaws, a small voice whispered in his brain. Because you want what other men have—a woman who loves you to come home to, a couple children to carry on your name, a legacy to leave behind that doesn't involve killing.

He'd noticed it more and more lately that he wasn't content with the way his life was going. He could start a herd of his own like his brother had, but he still wouldn't have what his brother had. He'd still be alone, and at least when he was out on the trail tracking outlaws, he didn't have to think about it too much.

CHAPTER 5

*H*annah stood at the entrance to the cave, soaking up the heat from the fire. She heard Kirby moving around inside, but didn't want to leave the warmth of the fire to see where he was.

"Here. This'll help you stay warm."

Kirby's voice came from right behind her. She spun around to face him as he wrapped his duster around her shoulders and overlapped the front, trapping her inside.

She laughed. The duster cocooned her, the hem dragging on the floor of the cave, the sleeves hanging to her knees. Still, she was grateful for its warmth.

Kirby walked away, and she turned back to the fire.

She hated that she'd had to depend on a man, but there were times when pride wasn't an option. She'd be eternally grateful Kirby had followed her from the ranch. She didn't know what she would have done without him. Probably freeze to death or be eaten by a wild animal, she reasoned. Either way, she likely would have died since she had no idea how to survive in the wilderness.

She glanced up at the night sky. The clouds were gone, the sky now a blanket of twinkling stars. A full moon shone down. Warmer now, she turned to see what Kirby was doing.

She didn't care what he was doing, she told herself. Yes, he'd been kind and gone out of his way to help her, but he'd only done what any decent man would have done.

Still, she couldn't help the strange feeling that settled in her chest whenever she looked at him. Or the strange heaviness low in her belly, almost an ache for something, but she had no idea what.

At the same time, she found she enjoyed looking at him, and though she was loath to admit it even to herself, she'd liked being in his arms, feeling his solid chest against hers.

She'd never experienced such sensations before, and it annoyed her.

Was this what Florence had meant when she'd told Hannah what love felt like? Surely she couldn't be falling in love with Kirby. Could she?

That wasn't possible. Not only did she barely know the man, even if she did, she wouldn't allow it. He's a lawman, she reminded herself.

Whatever feelings she was developing for him, she'd deal with them once she was in Silver City. She only had to get through tonight. Tomorrow they'd part ways and she'd never have to see him again.

She folded her arms across her chest, gazing absently at the flames licking at the wood.

Suddenly, a sharp sound split the air and splinters of rock showered down on her.

Her breath caught. Her brain stopped working.

Somebody had shot at her!

Kirby recognized the sound echoing in the air. A gunshot!

"What the—?"

He'd been near the back of the cave when the sound had echoed outside. He spun around to see Hannah standing at the entrance to the cave, facing out past the fire. Her face had lost all color, her eyes wide with fear.

His stomach clenched so tight his breath caught in his throat at the thought she might be hurt. "Hannah! Take cover!" he called out, dropping the bedroll he'd been untying from his saddle as he pulled his Colt 45 out of the holster at his side.

She didn't move until he grabbed her arm and dragged her into the safety of the cave. She gazed up at him, her eyes glazed with fear as if her brain was addled. Her balance faltered and she fell hard against him. Her fingers clutched at the front of his shirt, and he wrapped his arms around her and pulled her close.

Her scent filled his nose, and her quick shuddery breaths puffed against his neck.

"Are you all right?" he asked. He tried to keep his voice calm, but he couldn't quite manage to hide the fear surging through him. If anything happened to her … His stomach tumbled and his chest constricted in his own fear.

He didn't have time to think about his feelings right now. He had to keep her safe and then he needed to find out who was shooting at her, and why?

She nodded, but her lips had thinned and she was trembling in his arms. He didn't have time to sympathize with her right now, either.

She gazed up at him, her dark blue eyes filled with fear. He gave her a gentle shove. "Get your rifle, go to the back and stay there."

For a moment, she didn't move. He suspected she didn't like taking orders from anyone but in this case, he didn't have time to ask nicely. Then, she turned and limped away.

With his gun in hand, Kirby stayed close to the wall of the cave and approached the entrance, ready for whatever came.

Crouching down, he slipped out of the cave, keeping out of the firelight's glow to stay hidden as much as possible. He melted into the trees and peered into the darkness, searching for any movement at all.

He listened. The night was quiet, with only the sound of crickets to break the silence.

Nothing.

He waited, his nerves taut, his body tense.

A bullet whizzed past his head. He ducked behind a tree trunk. At least now he knew what direction the shot had come from.

His foot skittered on a pebble. He reached down and picked it up, then threw it into a tree a few feet away. The leaves rustled.

Another shot burst into the night. Metal glinted in the moonlight. He fired at it.

He thought he heard a mangled sound, but couldn't be sure.

He expected more shots, but none came, and soon after, he heard stones scattering in the distance.

Instinct told him the sounds he'd heard were made by the shooter's horse riding away. Still, he waited for what seemed like hours before he picked his way back to the cave.

Questions tumbled through his brain. Who'd tried to kill Hannah? And why?

The realization hit him swiftly. Hannah wasn't the target. He was. In the shadows, with Hannah wearing his duster, the shooter had made a mistake.

And if Kirby was a betting man, he'd bet the man holding that gun was Owen Cooper, Abel's brother.

He shouldn't be surprised Owen Cooper would try to kill him. Kirby had killed one Cooper brother and was on his way to testify against the other. He should have known Owen would come after him.

But he hadn't thought of it, and because he

hadn't, Hannah could have died. Guilt surged through him.

Hannah was perched on one of the rocks in the back corner of the cave, her rifle aimed at the roof. Her face was pale and he noticed she was still trembling, but she gave him a tiny smile when he approached.

"Whoever it was is gone now," he said softly. "You're safe."

"But why would somebody be shooting at me? I don't understand—"

Kirby gently gripped her shoulders and met her frightened gaze. "It's possible it might have been one of Abel Cooper's gang, but I'd say it's his brother, Owen."

A frown creased her forehead. "Why would he shoot at me? I have nothing to do with this trial you're testifying at, and I don't look at all like you."

Kirby let out a short laugh, his gaze drifting from her hair to the tips of her toes. "No, you don't. He'd have to be blind to think there's any resemblance at all between you and me. You're a lot prettier than I am."

She chuckled, the soft melodic sound sending waves of heat through his veins.

"But," he went on, "it's dark out there and you were standing in the shadows. Not to mention you're wearing my duster."

"Oh … of course … but why do you think it's Owen and not one of the others?"

"The Cooper boys are a close-knit bunch, and

they're the kind of men who wouldn't be satisfied letting somebody else get revenge for them. I killed Jubel Cooper, the youngest brother, and since Abel's in jail, it's up to Owen make me pay for it."

"So he could have killed me by mistake?"

Kirby nodded. "I'm afraid so."

"But he's gone now?" she asked. Her voice trembled slightly.

"I'm pretty sure he is," Kirby replied. "I think I wounded him, and I thought I heard some stones and pebbles skittering off the trail. Could be he was riding away."

"I hope so."

"Don't worry. We're safe, at least for now."

Hannah nodded, but Kirby wasn't sure she believed him. He crossed to where he'd dropped the bedroll at the first shot. He picked it up and shook it out, then spread it on the ground. "I don't have a pillow for you, but you should be warm enough."

"I'm not taking your bedroll—"

"I'm fine right here," he insisted, sliding down the wall near the entrance to the cave. With his knees bent, he leaned against the wall, his gun in his hand draped over his knee. "You should get some sleep," he said.

"What about you?"

"I'm not tired right now," he said. "I'll keep watch."

She looked as if she was about to protest, but thought better of it. "Then wake me when you get tired and I'll take over," she said. "I do know how to use a rifle," she added with a tremulous smile.

The lie slipped easily from his lips. "I will."

Hannah woke, the gray light of dawn seeping into the opening of the cave. The fire had died down during the night, but the embers still glowed bright red and a few persistent flames licked at the wood.

Kirby had been right. Although the fire had been built outside, it had generated enough heat to warm the inside of the cave enough to be comfortable in Kirby's bedroll.

Her gaze slid immediately to Kirby. He still sat against the wall, his gun in his hand, his eyes trained on the entrance. "You didn't wake me," she said quietly.

He turned his head to face her. "Good morning."

Hannah climbed out of the bedroll, smoothing the wrinkles in her dress as she crossed to him. "Why didn't you wake me? I fully intended to take my turn keeping watch."

His lips curved in a smile. "I know that, but if you remember, I said I'd wake you when I got tired. I didn't get tired."

"That's impossible," she sputtered. "You can't stay awake all night and not be tired—'

"I've had lots of practice." He climbed to his feet and brushed the dust and dirt off his pants.

The fire had burned out at some point during the night, but Hannah had slept so soundly she hadn't noticed.

She watched as he strolled to the entrance of the cave, his gaze sweeping the surroundings outside. She noticed he was favoring one leg.

"Are you hurt?" she asked.

He looked at her as if he didn't know what she meant before he saw her gaze resting on his knee. "No," he said. "It's an old injury. It's a little stiff from sitting in the same position for too long, that's all."

"Why? What happened to it?"

As soon as she asked the question, she regretted it. She shouldn't get to know him. Knowing him would make it far too easy to care about him. And caring was the last thing she wanted to do. He'd be gone from her life in a few hours, and that's the way she wanted it.

"A stray bullet," he answered quietly. "I was lucky it didn't shatter my knee completely."

Yet another instance of how being involved with a lawman was not a good idea.

He reached into his saddlebag and pulled out the leftover cheese and bread from their meal the night before. He moved toward her and offered it to Hannah.

"No, thank you," she said. The less time she spent with him, the better. "I'm not hungry, and I'd like to leave as soon as possible."

He nodded in agreement, and they spent the next few minutes packing up what they'd used.

"We'd better ride the rest of the way separately," she said once the horses were saddled and they were ready to leave. She'd taken a few minutes to attend to her personal needs and to run a brush through her hair. Without the benefit of a mirror, it had been difficult to pin her hair in place, but she'd done the best she could.

When she'd returned, Kirby had slid his gaze over her, his eyes filled with desire and … lust. Yes, lust was the word she'd use to describe his heated gaze, a gaze that had made her body tingle and warmth seep through her veins and settle low in her belly.

"I don't want to arrive in Silver City so early in the morning accompanied by a man," she said abruptly, forcing her mind away from the way her heart was racing.

She already had to deal with scorn from some people because she was unmarried and earning her own living. Her reputation could never withstand the scandal of people thinking she'd been in a compromising situation.

"That's not a good idea," he told her. "Whoever shot at you last night might still be out there."

She considered that for a moment. "If that's the case, then he's going to shoot me whether you're beside me or not."

"That may be true, but together—"

"If in fact Abel Cooper's brother is after you or it's

someone else trying to kill me, if we're together we could both be killed. If we're apart, only one of us will be. It only makes sense to split up."

Kirby took off his hat and raked his fingers through his hair. He began to pace.

Hannah watched him. Apparently this was what he did when he was thinking. Finally, he stopped and faced her.

"I hate to say it, but you're right," he said. "The more I think about it, the more sure I am that it's me he wants. Like I said last night, if he wanted to kill you, he would have. I realize it's best if I'm not with you. You're safer alone than you are with me."

She nodded. "Then I'll leave now."

"Sure," he agreed. "No problem. I'm in no hurry, so you might as well go on ahead and I'll follow a bit later."

She nodded. "Thank you. I do think that would be best."

She walked over to where Dixie was saddled and waiting. She paused. The truth was, she didn't want to leave. Even knowing it was the worst thing she could do, she wanted to spend more time with Kirby. If only he wasn't a lawman …

But he was! She'd sworn never to end up like her mother. Was this how her mother had been caught? Had her mother loved her father so desperately that she'd been willing to wait and worry every time he left the house? Or had that come later?

She'd never asked her mother what her father did

for a living when they met. She made a mental note to ask Florence when she got home. Perhaps he'd been a store clerk or a farmer and became a lawman later, when her mother was already in love. Surely she hadn't married her father, knowing what her future would be like—worrying every minute of every day that we wouldn't come home. Until the day he didn't.

"When this is over, I'd really like to come and call on you, Hannah." Kirby's voice broke into her thoughts.

She looked at him, taking in the golden flecks in his eyes, the lines and planes of his face, the way his lips moved a little crookedly when he smiled. "It's really not a good idea."

"Why not?" he persisted.

"Because …"

"I know you don't dislike me as much as you want to."

She looked away. She didn't want to see the desire in his eyes, desire she felt as well, even if she didn't know exactly what it was she wanted. "I didn't say I dislike you—"

He closed the gap between them, cupping her chin and forcing her to look up at him. "Well, that's good to hear, because unless you tell me not to, I'm going to kiss you now."

She should move away, should stop him, but she couldn't force herself to move. And what was worse, she didn't want to.

For a long moment, their eyes met, the golden

flecks in his eyes glimmering as his face dipped to meet hers.

She'd never been kissed before, and she didn't know what she was supposed to do, but it didn't seem to matter to him. His eyes darkened, a fire building in the dark brown depths.

Hannah's heart thundered against her ribs, and she sucked in a breath, holding it as his mouth closed in on hers. Her body trembled with anticipation.

His lips gently touched hers so gently, yet it seared her to her core. He released her chin, moving his hand until she felt it on the nape of her neck, his fingers threading through the strands of hair she hadn't been able to contain with her hairpins.

His other arm wrapped around her and drew her firmly against him. Her soft curves fit perfectly against his hardness, and she couldn't tell if the heartbeat she felt was his or her own.

His scent washed over her, and her senses reeled as he deepened the kiss. She heard herself let out a soft moan.

Her body was on fire, and she didn't care. All she knew was that she didn't want it to ever end.

A crow squawking overhead broke the spell.

She pulled away, her breaths coming in ragged gasps. She gazed up at him, wondering if she held the same expression in her eyes.

"I'd like to take you to supper tonight," he said. "Please say you will."

"I thought you were riding straight to Denver today," she said.

"I can stay in Silver City overnight and still reach Denver in time for the trial tomorrow," he replied. "So, will you have supper with me?"

She wanted to refuse, but the words stuck in her throat. Because, God help her, she was falling in love with the one kind of man she'd sworn to herself to stay away from.

Kirby watched Hannah ride away. His brain told him he'd done the right thing by letting her go on alone. But his insides clenched at the possibility he was wrong, and that Hannah was the target.

If something happened to her … No! She'd be fine! Owen Cooper was after him, not her. Once Hannah was out of sight, he left Gypsy tethered to a tree and headed into the woods where the shots had come from the night before. It was cool and damp, the smell of decay filling his nose.

He had a general idea of which direction to look, and he slowly wove his way through the underbrush, looking for a sign that he'd reached the spot.

The search was painstakingly slow, and he had to squint to see clearly in the dim light. He was about to give up, thinking he must have gone off track or that he'd been wrong when he noticed what looked like dried blood on a tree branch.

He entered a small clearing, and when he parted two branches, he had a clear view of the mouth of the cave. The ground there had been disturbed and he saw footprints in the damp earth.

Looking closer, he noticed a few drops of blood on the ground leading away from the clearing. He followed, eventually exiting the woods where footprints and hoofprints had trampled the dirt.

Owen Cooper was gone. But for how long?

Kirby retraced his steps until he reached the spot where Gypsy was waiting. He mounted and rode off at canter, scanning his surroundings, searching for a flash of metal glinting in the morning sunshine.

He was exhausted, his body ached from sitting in the same position for hours, and he couldn't wait to reach the hotel in Denver for a hot meal and a real bed.

Where was Owen Cooper?

As he rode, his gaze drifted to the foothills at the base of a stand of mountains in the west. His land was just over the ridge. Rich pasture and with ample water. Waiting for him.

Waiting for him to finally decide he'd had enough of chasing after outlaws, breaking up saloon fights, and waiting for one gunslinger or another to call him out.

His family, what was left of it, was there, too. Every time Kirby stopped to visit, Shane, his older brother, asked him to stay. He always refused.

Today, for some reason he couldn't explain, the

temptation to forget about Denver and the Coopers was almost too hard to resist.

But if he didn't testify at Abel Cooper's trial, Abel might be set free and they'd continue to rob and kill.

No, he had no choice. He'd testify at the trial tomorrow, and his testimony would either keep Abel in prison for the rest of his life or see him hang.

But tonight … tonight he'd call on Hannah, take her to supper and see if the strange feelings that filled him whenever he thought about her were more than just lust. His body made it clear every time they touched that he wanted her in his bed. But somehow, he sensed there was something much stronger, much deeper.

Was this what love felt like? His brother had warned him that one day, some woman would make him want more than a quick roll in the hay. He'd find a woman he wanted to talk to, a woman he wanted to make happy, and woman who made him happy when they were together and who made him miserable when they were apart.

Was Hannah that woman? He didn't know, but he was anxious to find out.

annah jumped, startled by the knock at the door in the rooming house where she was spending the night before she had to report to the Grover mansion. Why, she couldn't say, since she was expecting Kirby and a quick glance at her timepiece told her he was only a minute early.

She should never have agreed to have supper with him. Getting to know him was dangerous. Not physically, although she might have thought otherwise the night before, but definitely emotionally. She couldn't afford to let herself to care about him more than she already did.

The moment she'd first opened her eyes after her fall and she'd seen his incredibly handsome face, she'd known he was a man who could break her heart if she let him.

His smile sent awareness shooting through her.

Need settled low in her belly at the slightest touch of his skin against hers. And when he kissed her … Heavens, just the memory of it was making her tingle and her blood heat.

It was more than physical attraction, though. He was kind, and considerate, and she felt safe when she was with him. He was easy to talk to, something she'd never experienced with any other man. And if he was anything but a lawman, she'd be pleased to have finally found a man she could love.

The knock sounded again, louder this time. Even knowing in her heart that spending more time with Kirby was a mistake, she opened the door.

"There's a gentleman here to see you." Mrs. Fergusson, the white-haired woman who owned the house, smiled, her plump face creasing into folds. "A very nice-looking gentleman, I might add."

"Thank you, Mrs. Fergusson," Hannah replied. "I'll be right down." She picked up a dark blue reticule that matched her dress, adjusted the feathery hat perched on her hair in the mirror above the dresser and then hurried down the stairs.

Her breath caught at the sight of him. He was incredibly handsome, even more so now that he'd obviously taken a bath and shaved. A whiff of a woodsy fragrance drifted to her nose.

"You look beautiful," he said, giving her an appraising glance.

Heat flushed her cheeks. A long hot bath had

worked wonders for her aching muscles, and at least now she felt clean again. She'd put on one of her favorite dresses, a dark blue gown with ruffles at the collar and cuffs, and a white ruffle around the hem. "Thank you," she murmured. "So do you."

His brows lifted and he grinned. "I look beautiful?"

"No … I meant … you look very …"

"Handsome? That's the word you were going to say, wasn't it?" he teased.

She chuckled. "Yes," she agreed. "You look very handsome."

"I clean up once in a while," he told her. "Shall we go?" He opened the door and stepped aside to allow her to leave first.

When they stepped outside, he held out his arm. She tucked her hand into the crook of his elbow. Somehow it felt very comfortable to be out walking with him in the twilight.

The restaurant was intimate, and the meal was delicious. They talked, the topics ranging from art to history to horses and ranching. Hannah couldn't remember ever feeling so relaxed in the company of a man. Still, she couldn't help worrying that the evening was a mistake.

There was no doubt now that she was falling in love with him. And that this would have to be the last time she'd see him.

Night had fallen by the time they left the restaurant with only lamplight to guide them back to the rooming house.

Carriages rolled by. Couples and groups of friends strolled down the street, and much as Hannah knew she should be glad, she found she was disappointed to arrive at the rooming house.

She stopped at the bottom of the stairs and turned to face him. "I … thank you for supper …"

In the lamplight, the gold flecks in his eyes gleamed. "I hope this isn't the last supper we'll share," he said.

She opened her mouth to tell him it would be, but she couldn't force the words past the tightness in her throat at the thought she'd never see him again.

"How long will you be in Silver City?" he asked.

"Two or three days, I think. No more than four."

"I see. Once the trial is over, I do have some other business to take care of but I'll call on you again when you're back home."

"Kirby, I—"

"Do you know how much I want to kiss you again right now?"

The desire in his voice sent a tingle coursing through her body.

"Since we're in public, it would create a scandal, so I'll restrain myself. Next time we're alone, though …"

He may not have spoken the promise, but she was well aware of what he intended. Heat swirled through her veins at the thought, and her breath quickened. "How long do you think the trial will take?"

He shrugged. "It's hard to say, but the evidence is strong, and with my testimony, it shouldn't take much time for the jury to convict him. I'd say it'll be over in a day or two. Then I'll call on you on my way back to Cedar Valley. I want us to get to know each other better."

He took her gloved hand and raised it to his lips. Even through the fabric, she could feel his heat. "Until next time," he said.

Hannah couldn't speak, couldn't turn him down. Instead, all she could do was nod and climb the stairs. She glanced back to see him smiling, the promise in his eyes as she went inside and closed the door behind her.

The Grovers' Renaissance-style mansion sat high on a hill overlooking Silver City. The wealthiest family in the area, they owned the majority of the businesses in town, and Hannah considered herself very fortunate that she'd been asked to paint Mrs. Grover's mother's childhood home. The Grovers had a great deal of influence in this part of the territory, which could help her career tremendously.

She didn't like to be away from her family and the ranch, but the compensation Mrs. Grover had offered her was more money than she'd earn in years back in Rocky Ridge, and it would go a long way toward helping Florence and Archie to expand the ranch. In some small way, she hoped it would repay them a little for taking her in and supporting her all these years after her mother died.

Hannah stood at her easel in the solarium, where leaded glass windows looked out over a vast green lawn. She studied the painting on the easel, trying to decide if she should add more detail to the roof of the house on the canvas. The photograph she'd used to create the painting was in shades of gray, and she wasn't sure the colors she'd used were correct.

Her thoughts strayed back to Kirby's pronouncement. She should be furious that he'd just decided to come and see her without even asking permission, but much as she tried, she couldn't.

It had been three days since she'd seen him, yet she hadn't been able to put him out of her mind. During the daylight hours, she'd kept herself busy working on the painting. The nights, however, were long.

On Hannah's first trip to Silver City, she'd been given a bedroom in the Grover mansion that was larger than the whole house back at the Circle J. The four-poster bed had a down-filled mattress and was covered in silk linens and a heavy down-filled comforter.

Hannah had never had such luxurious sleeping quarters that she'd slept better than she ever had. This time, though, sleep eluded her. She lay awake each night watching the hands on the clock shift until finally she drifted off into a semi-awake state where Kirby's face filled her mind. She could almost feel his lips on hers, his arms around her, his hard body pressed against hers. Then she'd wake, her skin tingling, her breathing shallow and quick, and her body aching.

"You seem distracted, dear." Mrs. Grover's soft Southern accent filtered into her thoughts.

Distracted, unfocused, scattered. Any of those words would be fitting. "Oh … I …"

"Is everything all right? You're not still in pain from your accident, are you?"

Hannah had told Mrs. Grover about being thrown from her horse when the woman had noticed the scrapes and bruises on her. Hannah shook her head. "No. I'm fine now unless I stand for too long." Her scratches were healing well and soon, there would be no sign that she'd been hurt at all.

"Could it be a young man who's the cause, then?" Mrs. Grover asked.

Hannah felt a flush rising in her cheeks.

Mrs. Grover chuckled. "I thought so." She crossed the marble floor and stood beside Hannah. "I won't pry, but if you need to talk …"

"Thank you, but it'll all work out, I'm sure." She had no idea how she and Kirby could work out their differences, but she didn't feel comfortable getting into a discussion about it with her client.

The canvas on the easel was facing away from Mrs. Grover, so it was hidden from where she was standing. "May I see what progress you've made?" she asked, taking a few steps forward. Then she paused, waiting for Hannah to give her permission to come and look.

"Of course," Hannah said with a smile. "I think it's finished, unless you see something that isn't right."

Mrs. Grover rounded the easel, stopping in front and gazing at the canvas. Her eyes widened, and a hand rose to her lips. She didn't say a word, just stared at it. Silence filled the room.

Hannah watched the expression on Mrs. Grover's face, her nerves on edge. Were those tears in the woman's eyes? Did she hate it so much that it made her cry?

Hannah's heart dropped.

Then a moment later, Mrs. Grover looked at her and excitement her eyes glistened with excitement. "It's perfect," she gushed. "The way you've captured the colors, I can practically see the grass swaying in the summer breeze. I can't tell you how happy I am. My mother will be thrilled."

Hannah hadn't realized she'd been holding her breath, waiting for Mrs. Grover's approval. She let it out on a whoosh.

Mrs. Grover eyed her curiously. "Were you so worried I wouldn't like your work?"

Hannah laughed softly. "To be honest, yes, I was.

It's important to me that my clients are pleased when I'm finished."

"There's no need to worry," the woman said. "I love it, and I'll be telling all my friends how talented you are."

Hannah blushed again, but this time it was because of the compliment, not because she'd been caught thinking about Kirby.

"I'm sure you want to get home to your family," Mrs. Grover said, moving toward the door. "I do have some errands to run this afternoon so while I'm out, I'll go to the bank. If you don't mind waiting until tomorrow to leave, I'll have a bank draft for you when I get back."

"Thank you, Mrs. Grover," Hannah said. "I'm glad you're satisfied."

Mrs. Grover turned back and came to rest a hand on Hannah's arm. "I couldn't be happier with your work, dear. I suspect within a short time, you'll be spending so much time in Silver City that you'll have to move here permanently." Then she turned and left the room.

Live in Silver City? She couldn't imagine it. Hannah knew she should be thrilled by Mrs. Grover's reaction to the painting, and she appreciated the woman's enthusiasm and support. But leaving the ranch permanently? That was something she'd never even considered. Rocky Ridge was home, where her family was. Could she really be happy here? Alone?

And what about Kirby? She barely knew him, yet

already, she couldn't envision her life without him in it. Could she live here without Kirby? Her breath caught in her throat. The answer was simple. She couldn't.

The man who'd been elected to be the jury foreman at Abel Cooper's trial scrubbed at his beard for a moment before he swallowed loudly and read the words on the piece of paper in his hand. "We find the defendant … guilty."

The courtroom burst into chaos. Kirby watched as the color drained from Abel's face and he slumped into the chair in the courtroom.

The judge began to speak, but Kirby didn't need to hear anything else. The trial had taken longer than he'd expected, but finally, because of his testimony, justice was being served. Abel Cooper would likely hang for his crimes, but Kirby had no reason to stay for the sentencing.

He'd done his job, and now he had somewhere important to go. He stood and began weaving his way through the crowded courtroom.

"Matheson!"

Kirby spun around.

Abel Cooper glared at him, the hatred in his eyes almost palpable.

"You're a dead man," Abel's scratchy voice shouted. The courtroom silenced. "But before you die, you're going to know what it's like to lose your brother the way I lost mine. And as for his wife and those daughters of his—"

Kirby didn't need to hear the rest. "Shut up, Cooper!"

"And that little yellow-haired filly you've been with …" He grinned. Pure evil shone in his eyes.

Kirby's heart skipped a beat. How had Abel heard about Hannah? The only person who was even aware of Hannah was the man who'd shot at him. Had Owen Cooper somehow managed to get word to Abel? He made a mental note to find out who'd visited Abel in the past few days.

Two men dragged Cooper away, his taunts still filling the air even after the door closed behind them.

Kirby scanned the spectators in the courtroom. Were some of them Cooper's relatives? How else could he have found out about Hannah? Had he risked her life without even knowing?

He'd been anxious for the trial to be over so he could go back and call on Hannah, see if what he felt for her was real. He'd never given much thought to taking a wife, to having children, to having a family to grow old with until lately. It seemed that fate had brought Hannah to him at just the right time when he was already thinking about settling down.

If he'd met her a few years back, he was too young, too eager for adventure. But now … the time was right.

He wanted to go to Hannah today and tell her

how he felt, ask her if she was willing to give them a chance. But first, he had to warn his brother about Owen Cooper.

Hannah snapped the ends off another string bean and tossed it into the bowl on the table. She was both annoyed and worried at the same time.

She'd been back at the Circle J for almost a week and still hadn't heard from Kirby. Surely the trial was over by now, she thought, and if Kirby was really going to come calling, he should have been here by now.

She should be glad. And she was. At least that's what she'd been telling herself since she left Silver City and rode back to the Circle J.

Still, she couldn't get the thought out of her mind that something had happened, that he hadn't stayed away just because he'd changed his mind.

The way he'd kissed her … He'd felt it, the connection between them.

No, she was sure he hadn't changed his mind. Which meant only one thing. Something must have happened to him. Had Owen Cooper found him?

Her heart twisted inside her chest. Was he …? She couldn't even bring herself to let the word into her brain.

Stop it! she admonished herself. He was just busy.

He'd just been delayed. Nothing more. Surely if she kept telling herself that, she'd be fine.

So far, it hadn't worked. She barely slept, her appetite was gone, and she couldn't focus. Whenever she'd needed an escape from reality in the past, she'd been able to lose herself in her art. She'd go off with a pencil and paper and draw for hours, leaving the real word behind.

The day before, she'd gone back to the waterfall. This time, though, her fingers refused to listen to her brain.

"Are you mad at those beans?" Florence's voice reached her from where she was stirring a pot on the stove.

Hannah looked up. "What … oh …" She grinned, realizing she was throwing the beans into the bowl with a bit more force than was necessary.

"What's wrong?" Florence asked. "You haven't been yourself since you got back from Silver City."

"Nothing's wrong," Hannah replied, adding another bean to the bowl, gentler this time. "Really, I'm fine."

"You don't have to live in Silver City if you don't want to," Florence went on. "You can stay here as long as you want to. I hope you know that."

Hannah had told Florence how pleased Mrs. Grover had been with the painting as well as her predictions for Hannah's future. "I do, and I appreciate it."

"That's not it, though, is it?"

"What? It's nothing."

Florence set the spoon on a plate beside the stove and came to sit at the table. She reached out and squeezed Hannah's hand. "I know what worry looks like, and what it feels like. You can deny it until the cows come home, but you know it's true. Why don't you tell me about it?"

Florence had always been the one person in her life Hannah could confide in. Until now. Somehow Hannah couldn't bring herself to tell her sister about her night in the cave with Kirby, about her brush with death. And most of all, about the kiss they'd shared.

Why she'd kept it to herself, she couldn't say. It wasn't that Florence would be shocked. In fact, she suspected Florence would be pleased to see that she and the marshal were more than friendly.

Hannah wanted to confide in Florence that she thought she might be falling in love with Kirby, but she knew her sister wouldn't understand why she'd be so conflicted about it.

But Florence hadn't had to watch her mother die a little more every day after her father died. Florence hadn't had to listen to her mother's sobs every night as she lay in bed dealing with her own grief. And Florence hadn't failed to give her mother a reason for living again because the man she'd loved—the lawman she'd loved—had died.

No, she had to keep it to herself. That kiss had changed everything, and she couldn't explain it to Florence when she hadn't made sense of it herself.

How could one kiss make a person start dreaming about weddings, and babies, and … other things no decent single woman should be thinking about?

Hannah's stomach churned. The truth was, she was worried about him.

For the first time in her life, she understood how her mother had felt every time her father left the house.

Never before had Hannah felt this overwhelming fear. It filled every cell of her body.

She'd become her mother.

An unladylike word slipped past her lips.

Florence's brows arched and a tiny smile quirked her lips, but she said nothing, just patted Hannah's hand. "When you're ready to talk about it, I'm ready to listen."

Hannah gave her sister a small smile. "I know."

The sound of hoofbeats outside made Hannah's heart skitter behind her ribs.

"That must be Archie," Florence said.

Hannah's heart sank. She'd forgotten Archie had gone into town that morning.

"I hope he remembered to get flour," Florence added. "He didn't write it down and you know how forgetful he is."

Hannah tried to smile. "I do," she said, snapping the ends off another bean and tossing it into the bowl.

Florence grinned. "Hmm … even if Archie did remember to buy everything I asked him to, I think we both could use some time away from the ranch. Why don't we to into town ourselves tomorrow?"

Hannah looked up at her sister. "I think that's a wonderful idea."

The door opened, and a shaft of light beamed across the plank floor.

Hannah looked up, expecting to see her brother-in-law come inside.

Her heart skipped a beat. Kirby stood inside the doorway, looking more handsome than ever.

CHAPTER 7

*H*e was alive!

For the first time in a week, Hannah felt as if she could take a deep breath.

It took every ounce of willpower Hannah had not to bound out of the chair and run into his arms.

She studied him, the way his dark hair tumbled onto his forehead when he took his hat off, his broad chest that had offered her warmth and safety when she'd snuggled up against it more than once, his narrow hips and long legs.

He smiled at her and took a step toward her, then noticed Florence standing at the stove. He stopped.

"Welcome back, Kirby," Hannah heard Florence say. "Please come in and sit down."

"Thank you, ma'am," Kirby replied.

His gaze met Hannah's. "It's nice to see you again, Hannah."

"I'm going to check on the children," Florence

put in. Her dress swished against the floor as she hurried from the room.

Kirby crossed to where Hannah was sitting and leaned over as if he intended to kiss her.

She jerked out of his way, the chair scraping across the floor.

He straightened.

While fear for his safety had consumed her only a few minutes before, now anger surged through her. She bounded out of the chair and stepped away from him. She stiffened. "Where have you been? Did the trial take all this time?"

He shook his head. "No," he replied. "I've been at my brother's ranch since it ended."

"I see." Hannah tried to rein in her temper. It usually took a great deal to make her angry, but right then, she was furious. She'd spent days terrified that he'd been injured—or worse—and he'd been visiting his brother. "Did it not occur to you that I might be concerned?"

"It did," he said quietly. "I had no way to reach you to tell you I'd be delayed. Is Archie here?"

"No, he isn't." She dug her hands into the pockets in her apron. Why was he so concerned about Archie's whereabouts? "Why are you changing the subject?" She heard the words come out of her mouth and realized how childish and petty she'd sounded. *Heavens, what is he doing to me?*

"Where's Archie?" he insisted. "It's important."

"So you aren't here to call on me after all."

"You're wrong. I'm definitely here to call on you, but first, I need to talk to Archie." He smiled, but it did nothing to appease her.

"He went to town," she said. "I'm not sure when—"

The creak of wagon wheels in the yard caught her attention. "I expect that's him now."

Florence came back into the room and hurried to the door to open it. "Good," she said with a smile, "it's Archie. Now we can have lunch. Hannah, would you mind setting the table?"

"How did the trial go, Kirby?" Archie asked while they were having their coffee after lunch.

The children had already eaten, Libbie had been put down for a nap and Tommy was out of earshot, playing with a toy train on the floor in the main room.

"That's what I wanted to talk to you all about," Kirby replied. He was sorry he had to tell them about Abel Cooper's threat, and the real possibility that Owen was planning to avenge Jubel's death at Kirby's hands. The guilt weighed heavily on his mind.

If he'd waited to leave Cedar Valley that day … if he hadn't tried to seek shelter from the storm … neither his brother's family nor Hannah and her family would be in danger now.

But if he'd waited, or hadn't come across the Circle J, Hannah might not be alive today.

He rested his arms on the table and gazed at the dark liquid in his cup, trying to come up with the easiest way to tell them their lives were in danger. "You know about what happened the night Hannah and I spent in the cave."

Color flooded Hannah's cheeks and her eyes widened in horror. Florence choked on a mouthful of coffee. Sputtering, she bounded up and rushed to fetch a towel.

Damn! Kirby thought. She hadn't told them.

A frown appeared between Archie's brows. "No, we don't know what happened," he said in a clipped voice. His gaze slid from Kirby to Hannah and back again. "Care to enlighten us?"

"Nothing happened," Hannah cried. "Not what you're thinking, anyway."

Florence came back to the table, flapping her hand in front of her face to cool herself. "Well, that's good to hear," she said.

Hannah noticed that the words came on a sigh.

"Then what did happen?" Archie asked.

Kirby noticed Hannah had clasped her hands in her lap and avoided his gaze while he explained how they'd ended up spending the night in the cave, and the attempt on his life.

"Are you sure it was Abel Cooper's brother?" Archie asked.

"I'd bet my badge on it," Kirby replied. "Especially after Abel was found guilty and he threatened my brother's family and Hannah."

"So far, there hasn't been any sign of him at my brother's ranch," he said, then turned his attention to Hannah. "That's why I didn't come immediately after the trial. I waited there for a few days. Shane assured me he and his men could handle any trouble that came, and sent me on my way here."

Archie got up. He raked a hand through his hair and scrubbed at his chin. "You say you wounded him?"

Kirby nodded. "I found what looked like blood around where I think he was hiding when he fired at me so I'm guessing I did. No idea how bad it was, but maybe it was enough." He didn't bother adding that he hoped it was enough to keep him away for good.

"Thanks for warning us," Archie said. "I'll set up some extra guards around the house. Don't worry. Me and the boys will keep an eye out. We'll keep Hannah safe."

"I know you will." Kirby got up and came around the table. "Hannah? Can I talk to you?"

She looked up at him, then turned to Florence. "I'll be back in a few minutes to help with the dishes." She got up and followed him through the house.

Hannah squinted into the bright sunlight as she stepped out onto the porch and closed the door behind them.

Her emotions whirled inside her. She couldn't tell

where one ended and another began. She was still furious with herself that she'd spent so much time and energy worrying about him. She was afraid. Archie would do his best to protect them all. She knew that. But what if he failed? Would Owen Cooper kill them to get to her?

She couldn't live with that kind of guilt.

While Kirby was explaining the situation to Archie and Florence, a plan was forming in Hannah's mind. There was only one way to keep them safe. She'd have to leave the Circle J.

"Are you all right?" Kirby asked.

She shook her head, unable to put her emotions into words. She'd have to leave her home, her family. She could go to Silver City, start a new life there. Mrs. Grover had practically assured her that she'd be able to earn a living there.

Kirby grinned, that disarming smile of his almost making her forget her resolve.

"I can see the wheels turning in there," he teased. "What's going on in that pretty mind of yours?"

She probably should tell Florence and Archie first, but there was no reason not to tell Kirby. "I'm leaving the Circle J," she said. "I'm going to live in Silver City."

"Denver? Why?"

"I can't stay here, knowing I might be putting Florence and Archie and the children in danger."

"I'm going to find Owen Cooper. He won't hurt you or your family."

Kirby closed the gap between them, and as he reached for her, she stepped away. "Please don't, Kirby."

He dropped his arms by his sides. "What is it, Hannah? Are you still angry with me?"

"No," she replied quietly. "I understand now why you didn't come right after the trial."

"That's good." He peered at her for a few moments as if he were trying to see into her soul. "So what's wrong then? Why won't you let me kiss you?"

"Because there's no future for us," she said softly. "It'll only make it harder to say goodbye."

He took her hand, burying it between both his. "There can be a future if you want there to be."

If only it was that simple.

She'd fallen in love with him. She barely knew him, but there was no question in her mind about it. She loved him more than she'd ever thought it was possible to love another person.

But she'd spent days filled with anguish and fear, her worry so intense it was a physical pain.

How could she make him understand that she couldn't live her life that way, waiting for him to come back from trailing one outlaw or another? Or even worse, waiting for someone to knock at the door and tell her he'd been gunned down? "No, there can't."

"Why not?"

"Because …" she began. "My father was a lawman, just like you. I grew up watching what that did to my mother, seeing the worry and fear in her eyes every second of every day he was away from the house. I listened to her crying herself to sleep at night, terrified he wouldn't come home. And then, one day, her nightmare came true. He'd been trailing some outlaw or another in the mountains and he was killed."

Kirby took her hand. "I'm sorry."

"I was devastated," she went on. "Eventually it stopped hurting so much and I could think of him with a smile instead of tears. I thought my mother would be the same, that once she got past her initial grief, she could be happy again since she wouldn't have to worry anymore." She let out a laugh. "That shows how much I knew about love. She never recovered from losing him. No matter what I, or Florence, or her friends did to try to help her, nothing worked. She lost interest in living. I tried to take care of her, but she didn't want to live without him. She gave up."

"She's gone now?" he asked.

Hannah nodded. "She died a few months after my father was killed."

"That's when you came to live with Florence and Archie?"

"I'm sure they felt sorry for me. The house we lived in had been provided by the town so I would have been homeless if I hadn't come here to live. I'll be forever grateful to them for taking me in. That's why I try to repay them and help out financially when I can."

Other than a few sparrows chirping in the trees,

silence fell between them. He moved away from her, leaned a hip against one of the porch railings. He cleared his throat, and then straightened. He strode to the other end of the porch, staring out at the pastures surrounding the house.

Hannah wished she knew what was going through his mind? Then he turned back to face Hannah. "You don't have to live in Silver City."

"Mrs. Grover—" she began.

"You can live with me," he said. His voice had an urgency to it she'd never heard before. "I know we don't know each other that well," he began, "but I'm pretty sure I'm falling in love with you. I want to marry you. I'll do it today if you want, or next week, or next month, whenever you're ready."

Hannah's eyes filled with tears, spilling over and trickling down her cheeks. "I'm pretty sure I love you, too."

He grinned, his eyes lighting up as if she'd offered him the world.

"But the answer is no."

The smile disappeared as quickly as it had appeared. "What? Why not?" he asked, a disbelieving tone in his voice.

"Don't you see?" she began. "I won't be like my mother. I won't spend my life worrying, waiting for that same knock at the door. Afraid."

"You think a doctor can't die, or a blacksmith, or a store clerk—?"

Her eyes narrowed and her lips thinned. "Don't

ridicule me. Of course I know anyone can die, but the chances are much higher when you spend your time tracking down men who have no qualms about killing."

"Doesn't it matter to you that I love you and you love me?"

"Of course, but …" She could barely speak past the lump in her throat and the ache in her chest. "I think it's best if you leave now."

He held his arms out to her, but she moved out of his reach. She had to be strong. It was better this way.

"Goodbye, Kirby," she said through her tears. "Please take care of yourself."

Taking a deep breath, she walked away from him and went into the house, collapsing against the door and letting her tears fall freely down her cheeks.

"Where's Kirby?"

Florence appeared in the kitchen doorway, wiping her hands on a dish towel. She stopped for a moment and peered at Hannah. "Are you crying?"

Hannah brushed at her tears and sniffled loudly. Raising her head, she met her sister's concerned look, hoping her tear-stained face and her red eyes wouldn't give her away. "No."

"Are you sure? You look a bit disheveled."

"Positive." Hannah moved toward the stairs. "I'll be down in a little while."

"Where did Kirby go?" her sister asked again. "Is he staying for supper? Overnight?"

Hannah's heart felt as if it had shredded inside her. All she wanted was to spend some time alone, to reassure herself she'd done the right thing, no matter how much it hurt right now. Yet she couldn't avoid her sister forever.

"He left," she said quietly.

"When is he coming back?"

Hannah's throat constricted. "He isn't. He's likely gone after Owen Cooper."

"But after—"

"He won't be back." Hannah couldn't contain her tears a second longer. Brushing past her sister, she raced up the stairs and into her bedroom. She slammed the door behind her and threw herself onto her bed, letting her tears flow.

"It's been pretty quiet since you left." Buck, Kirby's deputy, got up from the chair behind Kirby's desk. "Old man Featherstone got all riled up when some kids let his cows out and he had to go chase them down."

"Did you find out who did it?"

Buck shook his head. "No way to know for sure, but I have a feeling it was those new folks out Bear Creek way." He crossed the office to the pot-bellied stove in the corner, his spurs jangling with every step.

"That it?" Kirby asked, casually leafing through a pile of papers and wanted posters on the corner of his desk. He'd take a closer look later, once he'd caught up on everything that had happened since he left.

"… and some of the hands from the Lazy L got into a brawl with the hands from the Bar-J, but we got that calmed down quick enough before the bullets started flying."

"Good. Thanks for taking care of things while I was gone."

"No problem," Buck replied. He held up a chipped pottery mug. "Want one?"

Kirby nodded. Buck filled the mug with steaming coffee and brought him the mug, then went back to pour one for himself.

"So how did the trial go?" Buck asked as he came and slouched in a chair facing Kirby's desk. "Did Cooper get convicted?"

"The jury was out for less than an hour," he said after he'd finished telling Buck the details of his trip to Denver, omitting any mention of Hannah or her family. "I need you to keep an extra eye out for Owen, though."

"Owen?"

"I'm almost positive it was Owen who shot at me, and Abel swore Owen was going to kill me, my brother and … I think I wounded him that night, so that might be why he hasn't come after me yet. If I'm lucky, he's already dead. If not, I'm going after him. I need you to keep things under control here."

"Sure thing, Kirby," Buck said. "You don't have to worry about anything here."

"Good. I'll head out first thing in the morning." Kirby picked up his hat and planted it on his head. Then he opened the office door. "Right now, I'm going to take a walk around town. I'll meet you over at the café in a half hour for supper."

CHAPTER 8

Hannah sat on the porch, her drawing pad in her lap. She stared down at the blank paper and at the pastel in her fingers.

What was wrong with her? She'd never been unable to draw, never felt this complete lack of desire to make images on paper or canvas.

Art was part of her soul, of her very being. It had been as far back as she could remember. Without it, who was she?

The door opened and she looked up. Florence stood in the entrance, a tray holding a plate of cookies and a glass of milk in her hand. "Cookies and milk might make you feel better."

"Thanks, but I'm not really hungry," Hannah said.

Florence set the tray on the table between the two rocking chairs that sat on the porch. She sat down in the chair beside the one Hannah was gently rocking. "You can't go on like this, Hannah."

Hannah gazed out over the fields. She hated that her sister was concerned about her, but she couldn't shake the sadness that seemed to have infected every part of her. She plastered a bright smile on her face. "I'm fine. Really."

"You shouldn't have sent Kirby away," Florence said.

Hannah shifted to face her sister. It had taken her three days to finally admit to Florence that she'd asked Kirby to leave and that he was off somewhere tracking down a killer. "I had to," she replied. "You know that."

"Because you're scared you'll end up like Mama."

Hannah nodded. "I can't spend my days afraid that he won't come home like Mama did."

"You're forgetting one thing, Hannah." Florence reached out and clasped Hannah's hand. "You're not Mama. You're stronger than she was."

"No—"

"Yes!" Florence interrupted. "You are. You weren't born when Papa became sheriff. I was, and I remember Mama before he took the job. She was the same even then. She'd burst into tears if he left the house for more than a few minutes. She was terrified to be alone. When he was offered the job as sheriff, she threatened to leave him. I was supposed to be sleeping, but I heard them arguing so I crept out of bed and hid at the top of the stairs. I watched through the railings."

Hannah was stunned. She'd never known about any of this. "But she didn't leave."

"No, she didn't." Florence picked up the glass of milk, offered it to Hannah, then took a long drink when Hannah shook her head. "She told him then that she'd never loved him, that the only reason she'd married him was because she wanted security and someone to look after her. That if he wasn't going to be there to provide it, she'd leave."

"I can't believe—"

"It's true," Florence continued. "He told her he was taking the job whether she liked it or not. I remember watching him walk over to the door and open it. It was winter, and the frigid air swept up the stairs. I was so cold, but I couldn't move. I was so afraid that Mama was going to leave me."

"What happened then?" Hannah asked, absently picking up a cookie and nibbling on it.

"He told her she was free to go, but that she'd be leaving alone. She wouldn't be taking me with her."

"So she stayed because of you."

Florence let out a laugh tinged with bitterness. "I wish that were true, but I don't think so. She stayed because her threat didn't work, and if she'd left, she wouldn't have any security at all. She couldn't look after herself."

"I had no idea …"

"Mama never loved Papa, even though after that, they didn't argue so much."

Memories washed over Hannah that now made perfect sense.

"Then how did I—?"

Florence let out a short chuckle. "I guess they tried to get along—once."

"When Papa became sheriff, her worry wasn't for his safety, but that if something happened to him, she'd be alone again. Nothing else."

Hannah got up and moved to the railing, looking out over the fields surrounding the house.

"You're not Mama," Florence said behind her. "You'll worry about Kirby when he's out doing his job, but that won't be any different than what you're doing now. There's one difference, though."

Hannah spun around to face her sister. "What's that?"

"Right now, you'll worry about him every minute of every day because you don't know where he is or what he's doing. If you were with him, there would be times when he was home with you that you wouldn't have to worry."

Hannah hadn't thought of it that way. It was true that worry and fear had eaten at her every waking moment since he'd ridden off. Even her sleep was fitful, waking every few minutes, her heart pounding.

She'd made a huge mistake. Having him with her part of the time was better than not having him at all. Yes, she'd worry when she was alone, but when they were together … she'd have joy and happiness instead of the sadness and misery she was living with now.

Reaching down, she grabbed her sister's hands and pulled her to her feet. She threw her arms around her and hugged her tightly. "Thank you for telling me about Mama. I wish I'd known before—"

"There was no reason to mention it while Mama was alive. I didn't want you to resent her when she needed you so badly."

"I understand," Hannah said.

Florence patted Hannah's hand, then picked up the tray. "I hope that makes you feel a little better," she said as she opened the door and went inside, leaving Hannah nibbling on a cookie and thinking about what she'd just learned.

And what she was going to do about it.

"Matheson!"

Kirby turned from the wanted posters he was nailing to the wall behind his desk. His stomach clenched at the tone in the voice coming from outside the office. He'd heard that tone before, right before some gunslinger or another called him out.

This time, though, something in him had changed. He wasn't a coward. He'd faced down men over the years when the odds were stacked against him surviving without giving it much thought.

But that was before he met Hannah. Now, he had

something to live for. Someone to live for, even if she had sent him away. Once he took care of Owen Cooper, he'd go back to the Circle J, and this time he wouldn't leave until she agreed to leave with him.

"Matheson!" the voice called out again. "You too yella to come out here and face me like a man?"

Kirby sighed, took his hat off the hook by the door, adjusted his gunbelt and stepped outside.

He squinted into the afternoon sun, pausing on the boardwalk until his eyes got accustomed to the blazing sunlight.

He could die today, he realized. He could die without ever seeing Hannah again, without feeling her touch, seeing her smile.

Owen Cooper stood in the middle of the street, his legs braced, his hand on the six-shooter on his hip. His hat shaded his face, so Kirby couldn't see into his eyes, but he didn't need to. He knew what he'd see there, a fire for revenge. And hatred.

How many more times was Kirby going to have deal with thieves and murderers before he took a bullet that would end his life? Until he met Hannah, he didn't really think about dying. Now …

"'Bout time you came out to face me," Owen called out.

"Are you here to give yourself up, Cooper?"

Owen laughed, a throaty sound. "You'd like that, wouldn't you, Marshal?"

"It would save your life," Kirby told him.

Owen took off his hat and wiped his forehead

with the sleeve of his shirt, then put his hat back on. "My life ain't worth much," he said. "Not with Jubel gone and Abel gonna hang. All because of you."

"You and your brothers brought it on yourself."

Owen laughed again. "Maybe you're right, but either way, I gotta kill you. An eye for an eye, the Bible says."

A tiny movement, and Kirby knew Owen was reaching for his gun.

Kirby drew his Colt and fired.

A moment later, Owen lay on the ground.

Two men hurried toward Owen. "He's dead," one called a few seconds later.

Hannah dismounted and looped Dixie's reins around the hitching post in front of the livery stable in Cedar Valley. A tall bald man came forward when she went inside. "Afternoon, ma'am," he said with a slight Scottish burr in his voice. "What can I do for you?"

"My horse needs feed and water and a stall for the night if you have one," she replied. "And can you tell me where I can find the marshal?"

"Right now, I expect he's at the saloon getting himself drunk."

Drunk? Hannah hadn't even considered the possibility that Kirby was a man who spent his evenings in a saloon.

As if the man could read Hannah's mind, he

added, "Marshal don't drink hardly ever, but when he has to defend himself with his gun, it does somethin' to him and he gets himself drunker than a skunk. Might not be that far gone yet, though, if you hurry on over there."

"Where might the saloon be?"

The blacksmith approached her. "There's three saloons in town, but you can likely find him at the Silver Dollar."

"Thank you," Hannah said, then hurried toward a two-story building about half way down the street. Three scantily clad women lounged on the balcony, calling out to cowboys as they passed.

As Hannah neared the batwing doors, piano music drifted toward her. "You looking for a job, honey?" one of the women called to her.

She looked up, her face flaming. "No." Then she spun around and pushed the saloon doors open and stepped inside.

Hannah had never seen the inside of a saloon. A long bar stretched the entire length of the saloon. Behind the bar, shelves held bottles of various sizes and shapes. A painting of a naked woman lying on a settee hung on the wall. She felt a flush of embarrassment creeping into her cheeks.

Several tables were spaced haphazardly throughout the large room. Men sat at some of the tables, and she noticed a group of men playing cards. A cloud of smoke hung in the air.

Piano music stopped. Voices faded.

As her eyes grew accustomed to the dim light inside, she saw Kirby sitting alone at a table near the back of the saloon.

He glanced up, his eyes widening when he saw her standing in the doorway.

Hannah's heart flipped in her chest. He looked so … Forlorn was the only word she could think of to describe the expression in his eyes. And sad.

Ignoring the men staring at her, she held her head high and marched toward Kirby's table. He stood, but there was no smile, no words of greeting. "What are you doing in here?"

How could she explain her change of heart? "I … we need to talk."

His voice was emotionless when he responded. "I don't see as we have anything to talk about," he said. "You made yourself pretty clear the other day."

"About that—"

"Not right now."

Had she made a mistake when she'd decided to go to him, to tell him she'd been wrong, that she wanted to spend her life with him? He certainly didn't seem pleased to see her. "Why not?" she asked.

"Because I don't feel much like talking."

It had taken a lot of soul-searching since the talk she'd had with Florence. She'd been willing to give up the man she loved because she was afraid she might lose him one day. But by sending him away, she'd lost him, anyway. She'd given up love, and happiness, and a family of her own. She'd given up the days and months and years she could have had with him because of something that *might* happen.

But what if it didn't? What if she didn't lose him?

When she'd realized how wrong she'd been, the decision had been easy.

And now, she was here. She'd come this far, and she wasn't going anywhere until she told him how she felt. If he wasn't interested, then she'd have to live with her mistake.

She planted herself in a chair at his table and set her reticule on the scarred wooden surface.

"You want something?" the bartender called to her.

Hannah was thirsty after her ride, but she had no idea what was available to drink in a saloon other than beer and whisky. "Do you have coffee?" she asked.

He nodded, and Hannah turned her attention back to Kirby.

"You should go," he said, staring at the amber liquid in the glass he had wrapped in his hands.

"I'm not leaving until you listen to what I have to say."

"Could be a while," he commented.

"I'll wait."

Soon, the other customers lost interest in her. The conversations resumed, and the tinny piano music started up again.

Hannah had consumed three cups of coffee

before Kirby finally spoke. "Come on," he said. "We sure as hell can't talk in here."

She got up. Kirby's hand cupped her elbow and ushered her outside.

Her eyes stung from the bright sunlight as he led her down the street to his office and stepped aside for her to enter.

He closed the door behind them and turned to face her. "What is it, Hannah? I'm in no mood—"

"I heard about what happened," she said softly.

"It was Owen Cooper," he said. "You don't have to worry about him anymore."

Hannah was surprised at the relief that washed over her. She hadn't admitted—even to herself—how terrified she'd been. "I confess I'm glad the threat is gone, but I'm sorry it had to end that way."

"It usually does," he muttered. He strode across the office and tore the wanted poster off the wall behind his desk. "Why are you here?"

"Because … because I was wrong."

His brows arched. "About what?"

"I was wrong to send you away," she said quietly.

"What?"

She repeated herself, louder this time. "I swore I'd never fall in love with a lawman, but it looks like I did, anyway."

"You did?"

She nodded, smiling softly.

"What about your mother?"

"I was wrong about that, too," she replied. "I'll

tell you about it another time. All I'll say now is that I'm not my mother. I know that now. So, do you still want to marry me?"

The clock on the wall ticked, filling the silence, echoing through the office as she waited for his answer. Her breath caught. Was he going to turn her away?

Finally, a grin spread across his face. "I sure do."

The air stilled. Her heart exploded with happiness. She closed the gap between them, tears of joy filling her eyes. She tried to blink them back, but gave up, smiling as they streamed down her face.

He pulled her into his arms, holding her so tightly she could feel his heart beating against her chest. Holding her as if he never wanted to let her go.

"We haven't known each other long," he whispered into her hair, "and I don't like the idea of a long engagement, but whenever you're ready … I most definitely do want to marry you."

Her heart was so full and her throat so tight with emotion it was hard to speak. While she'd hoped and prayed that he'd still want her, after refusing his proposal, a tiny part of her thought he might send her away.

Her voice trembled. "I don't believe in long engagements either."

He kissed her then, until they were both gasping for breath when he finally released her.

"I never expected to fall in love with a lawman, but I never expected to meet a man like you," she said, "and while I'll always worry when we're apart, I know you'll try to come home to me. That's all I can ask for."

"You know I'll do my best."

For a long time, they kissed, held each other, and whispered words of love to each other.

"I don't care where we get married, either here in Cedar Valley or in Rocky Ridge, as long as it's soon."

She looked up at him, at the intensity in his eyes, the way his hair tumbled down his forehead, and the smile on his lips She'd remember this moment forever. "The sooner the better."

EPILOGUE

 *wo months later*

"I now pronounce you husband a wife."

The preacher grinned at Hannah and Kirby. "You may kiss the bride," he said. Kirby cradled Hannah's face and lowered his lips to hers.

The kiss was soft and sweet, and over far too quickly, in Hannah's opinion. The crowd packed into the tiny church cheered as Hannah and Kirby made their way outside.

Although the wedding was being held in Rocky Ridge, it appeared that every resident in Cedar Valley had made the trip to see their marshal get married.

Congratulations and well wishes surrounded them, but in time, the guests wandered off to the hotel where a huge wedding feast was waiting.

"Don't you two take too long to get to the hotel so we can get this party started," Buck ordered. "I just got my eye on the woman I'm going to marry and I need to snatch her up before somebody else gets a notion to go after her."

Kirby laughed. "You go ahead, Buck. I have something to take care of first, but we'll be there soon."

Hannah was intrigued. What could he possibly have to do that was more important than their wedding feast?

"Come on." Kirby took her hand and helped her into the buggy waiting in front of the church. He climbed in beside her and flicked the reins, guiding the horse away from town toward the river.

"Where are we going?" she asked finally. "We have guests waiting for us."

"I'll stop soon," he replied. "I want you all to myself for a few minutes."

She shifted until her thigh was resting against his and tucked her hand beneath his elbow. Resting her head on his shoulder, she smiled. "That's a wonderful idea."

"I'm full of wonderful ideas," he said, reining in the horse and giving her a wide grin. "And surprises."

She straightened as he reached into his pocket and pulled out an envelope that had been opened and handed it to her.

"What's this?" She took the envelope and plucked out a single sheet of paper. Her eyes widened when she read the words on the page. She hadn't imagined her wedding day could get any better, but she'd been wrong.

"You really resigned?" She couldn't prevent the shock in her voice. "But—"

"I'd been thinking about it for a while, even before I met you. When Owen Cooper showed up, I knew then it was time. I almost got myself killed because of you."

"What? How—?"

"I was so busy thinking about maybe never seeing you again that I wasn't paying attention."

Hannah's chest constricted at the thought he might have died because of her. "What were you thinking about?"

"Oh, this and that," he replied. "Your eyes, your smile, your hair. The way you laugh. You're stubborn—"

She chuckled. "I like it when you're thinking about me, but not if it's going to get you killed. I'm glad you didn't die."

"Me too." Again, he reached into his pocket and pulled out a piece of paper. "I have one more surprise."

"Another?" She took the paper from his hand and read it.

"If you agree, I'd like to build a ranch on the piece of land my father left me," he began. "I'll build us a house, and make sure you have a place with plenty of light where you can draw and paint, too.

I've been saving for quite a while now, and this is a promissory note from the bank for the rest of the money to buy my first herd."

"The land near your brother and his family?"

He nodded. "I know it's not right near your family, but we could visit often. I'll build the house with plenty of rooms for company so they can come and visit us, too."

Hannah reached up and kissed him. She couldn't believe how much her life had changed, how much it was about to change. If she hadn't gone out to the waterfall that day …

He gazed down at her. "How do you feel about being a rancher's wife?"

She grinned. "I'd love to be a rancher's wife."

"I'm glad to hear it," he said. "You won't change your mind?"

She shook her head. "It might have taken me a while to change my mind about falling in love with a lawman, but I'll never change my mind about one thing."

"What's that?" he asked.

She reached up and kissed him. "I will never stop loving you."

Kirby was her life, her future, and whether he was a lawman or a rancher, she knew she would love him forever, no matter what.

ABOUT THE AUTHOR

Margery Scott is the author of more than thirty sweet historical western romance novels, novellas and short stories in various genres. Although she grew up as far away from the old west as possible, Margery has always admired the men and women who settled the untamed land west of the Mississippi. Glued to TV westerns like Maverick, Rawhide and Gunsmoke, and reading stories about Annie Oakley, Roy Rogers and Rin Tin Tin, it was only natural that when she started writing, she wrote what she loved to watch and read.

She now lives on a lake in Canada with her husband, and when she's not writing or traveling in search of the perfect setting for her next novel, you can usually find her wielding a pair of knitting needles or a pool cue.

Website: www.margeryscott.com
Email: margery@margeryscott.com
Newsletter: www.margeryscott.com/newsletter
VIP Facebook reader group:
www.facebook.com/groups/margeryscott